MW01241982

BLOOD, BODY AND MIND

AARON'S KISS SERIES BOOK 1

KATHI S. BARTON

This is a work of fiction. Names, characters, places, and incidents are products of the author's imagination or are used fictitiously and are not to be construed as real. Any resemblance to actual events, locations, organizations, or persons, living or dead, is entirely coincidental.

World Castle Publishing
Pensacola, Florida
Copyright © Kathi S. Barton 2011
Paperback ISBN: 9781939865199
eBook ISBN: 9781937593650
First Edition May 2011
2nd Edition World Castle Publishing December 1, 2011
3rd Edition World Castle Publishing, LLC August 15, 2013
http://www.worldcastlepublishing.com

Licensing Notes
All rights reserved. No part of this book may be used or reproduced in any manner whatsoever without written permission, except in the case of brief quotations embodied in articles and reviews.

Cover: Karen Fuller
Editor: Eric Johnston

DEDICATION

To Megan Pettet and Amanda McWhorter, the girls power reading my stories and encouraging me to write more.

To Erica Miller, the girl who keeps me smiling and laughing and looking good for the camera.

And mostly to my good friend, Phil Campbell. "Tahanks" for all the laughs and the great one-liners. That's the way we dose it!!!

Kathi S. Barton.

PROLOGUE

Melody looked at Marcus. She had never been so unsure of anything in all her considerable life. As queen, it wasn't something she wanted to happen again, either.

"Are you sure about this? She's just a child, not even a teenager yet. Why do you think this...this little girl has what hundreds — no, thousands — don't?"

Marcus, her Man at Arms of her Royal Guard, grinned. "Never been more sure of anything before, mistress. She's good — damn good, as a matter of fact. You should see her take down a man. Nothing prettier. She's even had the temerity to take me on a few times. Smart mouth, too." He grinned again. "You'll like her."

"I don't need to like her. It helps but is not...damn it, Marcus, I don't want a little girl getting killed trying to protect the kingdom." She moved through the portal into the human world. "We need someone who can follow orders, do as she's told, not a kid who's going to be a pain in my ass several hundred times a day."

They needed men. Not just men, but men of worth. Not to say that Melody had a problem with women defending the kingdom, but to the guard who served her, all were men regardless of their sex. They had put the magic beacon in the human world, hoping to attract some of those who would be able to serve. And so far, it had worked...to a point. There had been problems, issues with some of the others...others who couldn't be trusted with the secret of the Castle of Molavonta, The Magical Castle of her

Magick, Melody's magic.

Mel liked being the queen. She loved that she had the power of magic. *Hell,* she thought, *I am magic. All magic.* She governed the usage and the amounts used in both her world and that of the human world. There were creatures and peoples in her world that the humans wouldn't or couldn't understand. Dragons and unicorns, pixies and fairies, trolls and centaurs, and even kings and queens of all those, as well as princes and princesses. Mel had the best of both worlds. And as a true immortal, one who could never die, she had the added responsibility of keeping them all safe.

"All right then, let's go watch her. What was her name again?" They entered the large area surrounding the building and walked to the front door.

She could feel her own magic, the magic that kept all evil away and all those that entered safe from harm. She was comforted by it and what it represented. She looked over at Marcus when he didn't answer right away.

"Sara, mistress, her name is Sara Temple. And so you know…well, I've not told you something. Something that you will probably know soon enough."

She looked at him, dreading whatever it was he was about to say. "What is it, Marcus? Please tell me she's not a murderer or something. I'm going to be really pissed at you if she is."

"No, mistress, nothing like that. Well…why don't you go through the door and tell me? I swear to you, it will be a nice surprise." She didn't like what he was saying or the grin. But she did go into the large building, hoping that whatever it was wasn't going to piss Sherman off any more than he already was at her.

Her mate, Sherman, was mad because he felt he should be the one to gather the guard. Well, frankly, the guard didn't like him. Not only that but for some reason, she couldn't understand, they hated him. She didn't understand that, either. He was a good man if only a little self-absorbed. She did love him with all her heart. She and he had been mated for nearly a millennium now. She wanted to have his child, their daughter.

As the queen, it was decreed that she could only have a single child, a girl child who would rule when Mel was ready to step down. Her own mother had gone to Ireland some nine hundred years ago to fade, or to rest as a fairy ring, a magical circle of flowers that only the Irish could appreciate and love, with Mel's father. They would wake and come for a visit, but those visits had become less and less over the decades. She frowned when she wondered why. They were just to the door of the building when she felt the small bit of...something.

She glanced over at Marcus to find him staring at her. "It's her — the girl. The closer you get to her, the stronger it is. I felt it the first time I tangled with her. She has it hidden, but when she's fighting...well, she forgets to hide."

When they entered the large open area, Marcus excused himself to go and find the master. She had a chance to look around. It was a beautiful building filled with woods of every kind. She walked to the wooden post next to her and put her hand onto it. It was warm and gave off a feeling of peace and wellbeing. She gave the sturdy oak a bit of her magic, just enough to make him last, enough so that decades from now, he would stand and have knowledge that he stood for something other than a structure piece that some human needed to finish a project. The open walls and the wooden floors got the same bit of magic; warmth from her touch permeated the entire building before Marcus stepped back with her.

He stopped for a second, then threw back his head and laughed. "And how will the owner explain why this particular building still stands when all around it has crumbled?"

"I don't care so long as the people who enter here leave with the sense of worth and happiness." She took a deep breath. "Let's go and meet your friend so we can get back to the castle."

Marcus nodded toward a set of closed doors, and Mel followed him. Magic blasted her as soon as she stepped through the door. White magic, pure and barely touched, slapped her hard in the face. Beautiful and warm, it made her feel happiness, more than she'd given the post in the front and even more pure. This child's was untapped magic at its purest.

The girl stood in the middle of the room, surrounded by all the weaponry needed to train. She was tall for her age. Marcus had said she was just eleven years old. Mel wondered what her parents thought about her magic and remembered that Marcus had told her Sara was an orphan. Mel sat down as Marcus changed as he walked across the floor, his clothing of his guard's uniform fading away to that of a pair of worn jeans and a t-shirt.

"You're late, asshole. You said you'd be here an hour ago, and now I have a class." Her voice was hard, a direct contrast to the little girl standing so still in the middle of the room.

"I was detained. You think to teach me a lesson, child? I'm thinking you need your bottom paddled for the use of such language." When she snorted at Marcus, he continued. "Ah, you think I jest? No, I've come to teach you a thing or two about fighting. Have you studied the book I gave you from before?"

"Yeah, big deal. That book you gave me is really crap. There was nothing in there about what we talked about. I asked you how I get to have a sword that doesn't feel like I have to break an arm every time I want to lift it." She lifted the sword in her hand up to his face when he was close enough to almost touch her. "That's close enough."

The sword was too long for her. Even Mel could tell that. Mel closed her eyes and had one fashioned for her. All the child had to do was touch the handle, and the sword would be hers. Weight, balance, and even the length would be specifically fit for her. Mel reached out to Marcus mentally and asked him to give her the blade.

"Don't touch the handle. It will work only for the person who touches it. Tell her that you've had it made for her." Mel handed him the blade by the crown, and Marcus took it by the pommel.

She didn't think the child was going to take it, but when she looked over at Mel, she nodded once and wrapped her hand around it. Mel felt the connection immediately. Magic like hers poured through the connection, and Mel knew that Sara felt it, too.

"It's nice. Thanks," she said to Mel before turning back to Marcus. "Who's the broad?"

Mel nearly burst out laughing at the expression on Marcus's face. He'd been taught from birth to respect her as the queen. This chit had a few things to learn, the least of which would be respect if she made the cut.

"You'll keep a civil tongue in your head," he told her. "I told you before I was bringing someone. Now behave, or I'll take the flat of my blade to your bottom."

The girl snorted. "You can try old man. I'm not one of your rug rats to be ordered about. If you want to show off for your girlfriend, that's fine by me."

Her new blade sang through the air and sliced a tear in Marcus's shirt. The move was so quick Mel was surprised by it. Marcus only grinned.

"First blood." He bowed as he spoke. "Today, we fight for blood, not tears in our clothing. I'll give you this shot, but we go for good. Ready?"

"No. I won't hurt you. I refuse to play like this, so some woman will have sex with you." Sara dropped the blade to the floor as she spoke. "I told you before I'm only here because they'll feed me, and it's fun."

Marcus stood there with the girl, neither of them moving. Mel stood and walked toward them. Marcus was right; the closer one got to her, the stronger she was. She was standing next to her when she realized that the girl was reading her mind. Mel let her to a point but kept a great deal from her. She was not bad for a person without training, and Mel was equally impressed that Sara had such control.

"Hello. You're Sara Temple. I'm Melody, his queen." Mel nodded toward Marcus. "I want to show you something."

Mel turned to Marcus and took his arm into her hand. "Marcus is my guard, and as such, he can't be hurt by you. I can cut him." Mel sliced her own blade over his arm, drawing a line of blood. "But you—"

Mel was suddenly on the floor with a small, very sharp blade to her throat. The girl, Sara, was straddling her, holding her down.

"No," Mel warned Marcus when he drew back his sword to what Mel was sure to end Sara's life. "She was doing just what we need her for. Protecting one of my own."

"You were trying to prove a point? Wow, you're a real piece of work, lady." Sara stood and looked at her as Mel rose as well. "I'm so out of here. See you around, Marcus."

When Sara turned to leave, Mel stopped her with a question. "Sara, did you use your magic to throw me down, or was it your body? Either way was impressive. But I'm thinking you used your powers."

"I don't know what you're talking about. You're nuts. No one has magic." Sara still hadn't moved when she continued. "People would hurt someone if they had magic, don't you think?"

"Yes," Mel agreed. "But not where I'm from." Mel took a deep breath, tried another approach, and whispered through her mind. *"I can help you with it if you'll let me. I can show you how to control all of it."*

"In exchange for what? You going to slice open my head and see how my brain works? Tie me to a chair and put wires on me and shock me?" Mel felt her snort and nearly burst out laughing. *"No thanks, been there, done that."*

Mel wondered what else the girl had been through and then realized she would probably not tell her if she asked. "No, I don't need a blade to see what's in your head or your heart. Come with us, Sara. I swear to you, if you don't like it after one week, I'll bring you back and pay you for your time." Mel held her breath while she waited on Sara.

"You won't hurt me?" she asked as she turned.

"No, child, I won't hurt you." Mel put out her hand. "And so long as you're working for me, no one will ever hurt you again."

Sara nodded, then took Mel's hand. As soon as they touched, they were all three in Molavonta.

"Mother fuck," Sara said on a sigh. Marcus burst out laughing.

~~~

Fifteen Years Later

Aaron looked at his friend and day walker, Duncan, and wondered, not for the first time, what the hell he was doing. If Aaron lost this, then Duncan would die. He looked around the entrance hall again while he waited for Carlos Sanchez to receive him.

"Duncan, perhaps we should talk about this again. I don't think I can stand for you to—"

"Sire," Duncan began, exasperation in his voice. "I do believe we have re-mashed this several times already. I also believe that if you fail, you will be in no position to worry if I am dead as well. I do not believe that you will fail, but should you, then you will not even know that I have met my demise. You yourself will be ash and no longer aware of me anyway."

Aaron couldn't help it; he burst out laughing. "I suppose you're right. And it's rehash, not re-mash." They both turned as one to the doorway when they heard the footsteps coming toward them.

"You will do well, sire," Duncan said as he straightened the collar on Aaron's shirt. "This man needs to be removed from his position, and you are the man to do so."

Aaron nodded before they both turned toward the vampire

who had shown them in. He didn't look any better this time than he had the first time.

His hair was unkempt and lank-looking. His cheeks, his entire body, looked gaunt, and his skin, pasty white. He looked starved, and Aaron thought that for a vampire of this one's apparent age, it had to have been weeks since he'd last fed. But for all his sickliness, his uniform was in pristine order.

Clean and pressed, even his shoes were polished to a high glossy sheen. Like the house and its contents, money had been put into appearances and not into those that lived there. Aaron shook his head at the waste of money.

Carlos Sanchez had been the master vampire of this little realm for nearly three hundred years. Aaron had moved there several weeks earlier when a few meetings with some other vamps had told him what was going on. Aaron might not have thought the cruelty was true had it have been only one or two stories, but he had heard the same thing over a dozen times.

Carlos was abusing his position as master. Not only was he taking more than sixty-five percent of their total income, but he was not setting up anything in return for them. There were no health benefits for the human servants, nor was there anything set up for the orphans of vampires who were killed in fights or by humans. Then there was the physical abuse as well.

Starving them was bad enough, but he was also killing them. Murder of one's own kind was punishable by death. Only when challenged, could a vampire kill another. But he was killing for pleasure, to show others what would happen if they crossed him or tried to leave his realm.

As soon as they were led into the large receiving room, Aaron knew he had to win. The smell of death was everywhere, and the three dead women and the one man...all humans...on the floor before them were sickening, to say the least. Aaron gained strength in knowing that he would win for the people of the realm.

"Ah, Aaron MacManus. What brings you here tonight? Come to finally pledge to me, have you? It's about time. I was about to send out my troops to bring you in and make you do it." His laugh grated along Aaron's skin. "Well, my boy, let's get this over with."

"No, I have not. I've come to challenge you. Challenge you to your death for rules and rites of passage." Aaron drew his sword and slammed it deep within the carpeted floor, never taking his eyes from Carlos.

Carlos laughed again, but this time, Aaron could hear the forcefulness in it. "Surely you jest."

"I assure you that I do not. I, Aaron Xavier MacManus, pledged to no master, hereby challenge you, Carlos April Sanchez, to rules and rites of passage of this realm. I challenge you to your death."

Carlos looked at the men and women around him. Two of them stepped away and then flashed to the door and out of the room. One of the women made her way toward Aaron. He wasn't sure what her intent was, but she was stopped by Duncan, who simply stood in front of her, blocking her way.

"The last three times someone challenged me, I was the victor. You think you—"

"They were not me," Aaron said, cutting him off. He pulled his sword free and held it before him. "Are you afraid, Carlos? You should be, for I plan to make your death count for so much."

"You're going to regret this, MacManus. I haven't lost a fight yet, and I don't plan to do so to an insolent prick like you," Carlos snarled as he stood.

Aaron grinned and knew that Carlos could see no humor or friendliness in it. "So be it."

CHAPTER ONE

Sara paused only slightly when she felt it. Someone or some... thing had moved into her zone. As she continued to vacuum the carpet in the little Cessna, she reached out and touched the other people she knew to be inside the hangar. *Maybe,* she thought, *one of the others brought in a visitor.*

The mechanics, Mark and Tully, were in the outer bay; Maria, the cleaning lady, was in the waiting area, and the Carlovettis, Demetrius and April, were in their separate offices in the back of the hangar. No, they...because now she knew there were six... had come in as a group, and they were not with anyone that she already knew.

Sara Temple was an amazing telepath. Her ability to reach and search out those near was extremely strong and only one of the many and varied talents she had. She knew the building like the back of her hand, so she could also tell where they were headed or where they already were.

At first, she thought it was the High Council of Magick and that they had finally found her after four long years of hiding from them. Then she realized that had it been them, they would have simply materialized behind her, slit her throat, and then dematerialized again, all without leaving a trace of themselves behind to lead anyone back to them. That was the penalty for high treason and the presumed kidnapping of Queen Melody, Mistress of Light, Keeper of Magic—instant death. But she could not think of them right now, or of Mel, her friend. She needed to focus on the here and now.

No, their signature, or tag, was different. These...beings were not anyone she had encountered before. She was able to track them moving from the front of the building toward the offices to the rear of the large hangar.

Vampire — all six of them are bloodsuckers, she thought, *and by the signature, they are sending off, most are heavily armed.*

As she turned off the vacuum, she reached further, gently, so as not to alert those to her mind search, and looked to see why they might be there. She scanned each person separately to see what their intentions toward the Carlovettis were. She realized at that moment that they were not only there to kill the oldest vampire in their group but to blame Demetrius and April Carlovetti, her new bosses and the owners of the airliner where she worked, for his murder.

Sara was always armed, so she was well prepared to defend herself and others if need be. She was in constant danger from one source or another and lived in mortal terror because of it. She moved out of the plane easily enough and was on her way to the offices when she felt the presence of the new life. April was pregnant. Sara's sole purpose changed in that second. Now the need to protect April and the innocent life she carried became Sara's number one priority.

All of the vampire newcomers were older than both the Carlovettis, especially April, who had converted just a few weeks after she started working for them eight months ago. Sara had known all along that she worked for vamps, just as she knew that Charlie Wolff, her former boss, was a werewolf. She just chose to ignore it. It didn't matter to her what kind of being they were, as long as they did not snack on her.

As she moved along the building's outer walls, she kept her focus on any movements inside and around the offices that would alert her to sudden danger. She knew that one of the men was moving toward April's office where April was, so Sara picked up her pace. There were two more surrounding the oldest vampire. They were all with Demetrius, who was just inside the first set of rooms with the larger group, talking. She moved into the mind of Demetrius to see what was happening. It was easy; all she needed was a touch of bare skin, and she could usually talk to or read a person's mind. The conversation centered on the oldest vamp, the newest Master of the Realm, a man called Aaron MacManus, and what his plans were for his new realm.

Demetrius was wondering about the man's intentions in coming to the hangar without notice and seemed to have no idea that he was close to his own death.

The first vampire that Sara had encountered was still where she had felt him, standing outside the little reception area not ten feet from the others. He would have to be dealt with first and quickly. If she did not, then he would let the others know before she had a chance to try and save April and the babe.

As Sara moved toward him, she reached inside her left boot and pulled out a long, silver blade. It would not be considered a knife by most as it was just a one-inch strip of stainless steel with a fine coating of silver and a small handle that fit Sara's hand perfectly. Another blade lay hidden in her other boot. Down the back of her neck, a blade wider and longer by several inches awaited her usage. Two more blades, attached to bands up each sleeve of her shirt, were ready to be ejected into her hands when she applied pressure to her wrist.

Sara was surprised at his size when she saw him; he was very big. Tall, but that wasn't all; he was really fat. She had never seen a fat vamp before, and it surprised her. His thinning dark hair was pulled into a tight stringy mess at the back of his head. His dark suit fit him well enough, but she was sure that he would have a lot of difficulty if he were required to button the jacket. His tie was dark and matched the equally dark shirt he wore. He had on well worn, brown cowboy boots. But it was the automatic weapon he had resting across his arms that really drew her attention…not the weapon itself, but the fact that it had a silencer on it. Whatever they were going to do to the old vamp, they had no intentions of letting anyone else hear.

She was nearly to him, but at the very last second, the vamp turned toward her. She knew she had made a small noise to alert him; his hearing was very acute, like all vamps. Before he could react, she sliced his head from his body. Sara proved her blade and exceptional strength were better than any weapon he carried.

Sara crouched to catch his head as his body disintegrated before it hit the floor. His head followed his body seconds later, still receiving input as it had not yet realized that his body was gone. It took just a little longer. *Killing rogue vamps is not a messy job. Add a little silver, a little sunlight, and voila, nothing.* She nearly giggled out loud at this wayward thought. *It's better if I stay on guard,* she thought with a grimace.

Sara knew that one or all of the other vamps would feel him missing soon, if they had not already, so she moved forward into the room immediately, killing the next one as she came into the door in much the same manner as the first. Severing the head from a vampire was the only true way to kill them, and it was also the quickest.

Scanning the room with her mind, Sara located and sent a telepathic message to Demetrius to get to his wife, as she was in mortal danger.

"April is in danger. One of the rogues is headed toward her now. She is working in her office."

He did not even ask Sara how she knew or stopped to think about how she had communicated with him. He just flashed from the room toward his life mate.

When Sara looked back at the two remaining rogues, she saw that the fourth vampire had a gun pointed toward her and that the last had the older vamp by the throat and a jeweled silver dagger to his neck—Mexican standoff.

Mentally, Sara reached out to the hostage, not holding out

much hope that she could talk to him. "*Can you hear me?*"

"*Yes. Can you help me?*" he asked her. "*My name is Aaron MacManus. I'm the new Master Vampire in this realm.*"

Sara was pleasantly surprised to find he was open to her.

"*I only came in here to save the Carlovettis. That's done if Mr. Carlovetti can get to his mate in time.*" She focused on him for a second and said, "*He has her; she's safe now. I have no interest in you or saving you, Mr. MacManus.*"

She started to turn away when he stopped her. "*Wait, I'm asking for your help. What would it take to get you to save my life?*" he pleaded.

"*My death.*" She answered him quickly. *Death would be an end to so much,* she thought.

"*I can offer you eternal life, yes. You want to be an immortal. Done. But I must be alive to give you —*" She stopped him.

"*No. Death. Nothing more. I want my life to end. Today. If I save you, you'll end this life as I know it.*" When he agreed with a short nod, she moved slightly closer to her target.

Long minutes passed as Sara tried to reason with the closest rogue. She was making no progress with him; he had an assignment, and he wasn't deviating from it. *Plus,* she thought, *he is stupid. He has to know the others are dead, yet here he stands like he has a chance to get out alive.*

Sara knew that he was ready to strike against them seconds before he moved. She lunged forward, twisting around. She pulled the blade from between her shoulder blades and sliced the vamp with the gun in half at his midsection just as the gun went off. As the momentum of her twist brought her full circle, she dropped to a crouch and jabbed forward between the hostage's legs, severing the right leg of the vamp, and the last man dropped to the floor. This allowed the vampire, who had already proclaimed himself as master, to take out his captor by severing his head from his bleeding body with a quick morphing of his hand into a claw.

Sara, still on her knees, watched while he then proceeded to the vamp that she'd cut in half and dispatched him into nothingness as well.

As he moved toward her, she managed to stand again and bring her blade to the forefront, taking a stance that showed she still had a lot of fight left in her, even though, in reality, she was nearly done.

Blood was pouring out of the bullet wound at her side at an alarming rate. Adrenaline surging through her body, she hadn't even realized that she had been hit until that second. She knew that it had not hit any major organs, but that didn't mean it would not bleed for a while. Her body had an unnatural ability to heal itself very quickly up to the point where she was no longer in mortal danger. Major wounds would heal in a matter of hours rather than months, then she would heal like a normal human, weeks to heal deep bruises, and less if it was just cuts. As he moved within a foot of her, she brought the blade to his throat, stopping his progress. He showed her the jeweled dagger he had taken from the dead vamp in his open palm to show he meant her no harm.

"Do you truly wish to die, little warrior?" Aaron asked her.

"Yes, yes, I do. We had a deal, you and me. Mine for yours. Are you a man of your word, Mr. MacManus?"

Sara watched him bristle at that. *He is probably not used to having people refute him,* she thought with a grin.

The large vamp was very handsome, she realized. His hair was long and straight, hanging in a curtain of black halfway down his back. His face was beautiful, full lips, high cheekbones. His nose had a small bump in the middle like it had been broken once. That should have detracted from his good looks, but it only seemed to enhance them. His eyes were a startling shade of blue, the color so deep that they looked almost black. He towered over her five-eleven frame by as much as eight inches, and he weighed at least two-fifty. He looked fit; his dress shirt hung well across his broad shoulders and his pants hinted at muscled thighs and long legs.

Aaron stared at her too. He seemed to know she was assessing him. She flushed slightly when he grinned.

"Yes, I'm a man of my word. You still wish for me to kill you after you've just saved my life? You have no second thoughts?"

"It wasn't my intention to save you at all. I told you that. All I ask is that you make it quick and clean." She staggered slightly, dizzy for just a second.

"If we stand here long enough and debate the finer points of life and why you should live, you'll die anyway, I think."

Sara felt him try to touch her mind, and she tightened her shield. When he could not reach her, he continued.

"Why is it that I can see that you're bleeding, yet I smell no blood on you? I can't even pick up your human scent. Are you even human? I find that to be very curious." He looked her up and down, and she felt heat rush through her.

What right does he have to size me up? she thought. *It didn't matter about my size minutes ago when I was saving him. Arrogant bastard.* "Because I don't want you to be able to smell me, all right? That isn't what matters. What will it take, vamp, another attempt on your life? A stab to a vital area with a bit of silver? Tell me. We had a deal, yours for mine. Lop off my head and be done with it."

Demetrius and April chose that moment to enter the room. She felt their shock as though it were her own. Demetrius tried to reach through her shield, but she was a little busy.

"Master, she saved our lives. I beg for her life, sire. Without her, none of us, you included, would be here."

Sara chanced a glance over at him and frowned. She wanted to say, "Stay out of this. I helped you, now leave me alone."

"You beg for something that she is very willing, and wanting, to forfeit, Demetrius." Aaron nodded toward her. "Little Warrior here has asked me to take her from her subsistence. I haven't yet decided what to do about this."

Sara jerked back toward him. "We had a deal, damn it. Are you going to back out on your word? You said you could be trusted."

"Sara, drop your knife, I beg of you. He's my master. I cannot allow you to harm him, nor will I stand by and watch while he cuts your throat. Please, drop the knife and let us sort this out in a friendlier manner." She felt Demetrius move toward her after sliding April behind him as he did so.

"Demetrius," Aaron said tightly. "I would prefer that you wouldn't give her any more reason to cause me harm today. I've had a really shitty day so far. I've only just become master and would like very much not to be taken out by one small human. She would do it just to have you end her life, I believe. Wouldn't you?"

"I'll not cause Mr. Carlovetti any problems. I like him. But I tire of being a failure. There are people who would do the job you seem reluctant to do, but they wouldn't make it quick, I think. We can stand as we are while I bleed out, or I could kill you. It matters little to nothing to me."

She was getting weaker, and she thought he knew it too. If she passed out, she knew that he would not complete what he had promised…if his promises meant anything at all.

Sara had failed so many people. Her friend Mel had suffered the greatest loss. The queen had lost her unborn child, and it had left her magic weak, unable to protect herself from her mate, Sherman. Also, because of her failure as Mel's guard, she was being hunted by the High Council, the magick's governing panel within the magical realm of Molavonta.

Sherman would kill her. He had told her that often enough whenever he managed to find her. But she also thought that he would enjoy it too much and it wouldn't be quick.

"Drop the knife, and I will do as you ask. I will take away the life you live." Sara reached out and found that while Aaron was not happy with it, he was sincere in his promise.

Immediately, she dropped the knife. Its blade quivered in the wooden floor between them. The master took the last few steps toward her, bringing his body very close to hers, and he bought his hand to the back of her neck. He tilted it at an angle, bringing the long column of her neck up for his mouth and his very sharp fangs. She did not fight him or resist in any way. Closing her eyes, she relaxed against him.

Suddenly, she felt nothing as her world went black. Her last thought she sent to him was, "*Thank you.*"

CHAPTER TWO

"Master?"

Aaron had forgotten the man and woman behind him. He continued to look into the face of the woman in his arms. She was a quandary, and he loved puzzles.

"She's strong, isn't she? And stubborn. Who is she? What do you know about her?" he asked without turning around.

He did not want them to see him just yet. His eyes had turned; the need to feed from her was making him see her in a red haze. That and the touch of something more he wanted from her.

"Her name is Sara Temple. She is one of our pilots. Sire? I beg for her life, please? She saved our lives, all of our lives." April, too, was begging for Little Warrior's life.

Aaron had not met April yet, but he had heard a great deal about her from her mate tonight. Aaron guessed that she had been the reason Demetrius had left the room so quickly when the beauty had entered.

"Yes, as you have said before. I'm well aware of what she has done for us, and I have no intention of ending her life just yet, no matter how much or how prettily she begs. I have merely put her into a state of deep sleep until we can get her medical help. It is still a few hours until sunrise, and we have a lot to do. My car is just outside," Aaron decided quickly. "We will need to get her to my estate, and you two are coming with me. So I suggest that you make whatever arrangements you need to and do so now."

Aaron did not even turn around to see if they were doing

as he said. He was a man who was used to having his every command obeyed without question, and luckily, the Carlovettis understood that and jumped to do his bidding.

With the girl still in his arms, he leaned down to pick up her knife, careful not to touch the silver. Carrying his would-be killer, he walked to the big, black SUV and climbed into the back seat with her. He laid her gently across his lap as he pulled out his cell phone. He was just finishing his last call when the doors to his car opened in the front. The Carlovettis got in, Demetrius the driver.

Putting his cell phone away with a snap shut, he said, "I have contacted a doctor friend of mine, Thomas Reilly, who deals with humans as well as vamps. He will meet us at the mansion. What can you tell me about her?"

April looked over at her husband, then back at the vampire in the back seat. He was holding Sara in his arms and checking the wound while he waited for an answer. He looked up at April with a questioning expression.

"Do you plan to take her life, sire?" she asked him.

"Aaron."

Aaron wondered why they thought he would end her life so quickly or be so willing to do so. Then he thought of Carlos Sanchez, the former master of this realm, and realized that therein lay the problem.

As the way of vampire law, when Aaron had challenged the previous master for his realm, the two strong forces fought to the end. It had been a bloody and horrific battle, lasting nearly three hours—a very long time in vampire battles. In the end, Carlos was beheaded, and Aaron himself had been nearly mortally wounded. It took him almost a month for his energy and strength to be built back to what was normal for him. But of course, no one knew that for sure, and he wanted to keep it that way.

The winner, in this case, Aaron, had been declared the Master of the Realm, and he had been afforded all of the riches, property, and anything else the previous master owned, including subjects. *The loser?* In this case, Aaron wondered who had been the loser. *The realm was a total mess and —*

April's question pulled him from his thoughts. "I'm sorry?" Her confusion was evident in her tone.

"My name, it's Aaron MacManus. Please call me Aaron. And no, I don't, at least as long as she doesn't become a threat to us. You do realize that she single-handedly took out four rogue vampires without so much as a scratch on her? The bullet wound happened while she was begging for her life, or death, as it were, with me. She has abilities that go beyond a mere human; she walked up on all of us without anyone being the wiser. Surely you are aware of what that can mean to our race? To us?"

Aaron was in awe of her. His little warrior was as strong, if not stronger than, most men he knew.

"Yes, sire...err, Aaron. But if she wanted us dead, why would she have put herself in danger to save us in the first place? Unless...it was to cause her own death."

That was what Aaron was wondering too, and he was surprised that Demetrius thought the same thing. His estimation of the man's worth had just raised a few notches.

"Not us, just you two. She as much told me I was expendable in the large scheme of things. Her only objective was to save you. Why? I'd like to find out what makes a human feel the need to do what she did, to take such a chance." Or if she even was a human. He looked down at her again. "I take it she'd never given you any indication that she wanted death."

"No, never. There's something else you should know. I believe she sent me a hard mental push to go to April, saying she was in trouble. I never realized she was capable of anything like that, of telepathic behavior."

Aaron had thought as much when she'd kill the men with him. He had felt the small but strong mental push of compulsion but hadn't realized it had come from her. He looked up from her face when Demetrius continued.

"Honestly? There isn't much we know about her, especially in light of tonight's activities. We had no indication that she had these powers...abilities, I guess. I knew that I had been unable to penetrate her mind, but after trying hard for the first few months, then off and on over the last few, I just put it down as a natural phenomenon and didn't think much about it again. It happens in some humans, I guess. Now, it seems she is much stronger than I am, mentally, at least. I'm the best psychic I know...knew."

April picked up from Demetrius when he seemed to trail off. "She keeps to herself mostly. When we hired her, we were told that she's one of the best pilots that Charlie had ever worked with, even if you consider her young age. I'd have to agree with that after working with her."

"How long has she worked for you? And where did she work before? I'm assuming locally, right?" Aaron knew there were several small ports around the Zanesville area and one larger one in Columbus.

"I guess nearly a year now, just before April was changed." Aaron watched as Demetrius touched his mate and kissed her hand before he continued. "Her experience is vast and varied. She came to us directly through Charles Wolff, the retired alpha to the local were pack. She also worked for Columbus Airport as a substitute pilot or during peak times if they needed her. She flew their bigger planes, 747s and 750s. The local hospital used her as their chopper pilot about three or four times a month."

"What did she think about working for supernaturals?" he asked Demetrius.

Aaron was impressed with the girl so far, but that wasn't getting him any closer to figuring out what she was, only who she was. Aaron knew that he would not like the answer as soon as he saw Demetrius look over at his mate before replying.

"We didn't think that she knew what we are, any of us. Charlie told me that he thought she was unaware of what they were, and we assumed the same thing. I guess we were all wrong about her ability to know if we are immortals or not. He retired as their alpha when his grandson, Bradley Wolff, took over the pack at the same time that she came to work for us. Charlie said he knows you?" Demetrius said.

"So it would seem. Yes, I know of him and The Brotherhood of Gray, I believe. Why didn't she stay with them? I know they still have their own fleet. It seems if she is this good, they wouldn't have wanted to get rid of her." Alarmed by her sudden movement, he looked down at her pained expression even in her sleep.

Aaron knew that he could lick her wound closed, but he was sure that the bullet was still lodged into her ribs. If it were anything but silver, he would just dig it out and heal her. Then there was the added problem of what he suspected she might be to him.

"There was some bad blood between her and the grandson's wife, Lynne," April answered this time. "Charlie thought that she had always been very jealous of Sara and would have killed her if she had ever had the chance. Probably would have ended differently than he thought if today is any indication of her ability to defend herself." April laughed at her own joke and then sobered quickly.

Aaron sighed, wondering when they would feel comfortable around him. "Yes, I believe you're correct. I would like it if you two could stay at the estate for a while. I should have asked earlier and not demanded. She is going to be there for a little while until she's healed and will probably feel better about having someone she knows there. I don't have much in the way of staff yet, as I've only just gotten the house and ground cleaned up. But Duncan can see to everything you need." His tone was dismissive, just as he had meant it to be. He wanted to think—no, needed to think.

April nodded and turned back to face the front of the car. It looked as if he was going to be spending some up close and personal time with some of his new subjects.

Aaron waited until April had finished turning away before he looked down at the burden in his arms again. Sara was quite simply the most beautiful woman he had ever seen. And her smell…she smelled of calla lilies and honey. He was sure that the only reason he could smell her now was because she was in a vampire's sleep, deep as death.

Aaron ran his fingertip down the side of her face, marveling at the silkiness of her skin, the warmth that radiated from it. Her lashes swept out nearly a quarter of an inch across her high cheeks. Her brows arched beautifully over eyelids that, while now closed in sleep, covered the most startling shade of light blue he had ever seen, nearly clear in color. Her skin was the creamiest white, and freckles were sprinkled all over her small, upturned nose and the rosiest of cheeks, pale now because of her blood loss and other injuries. Her hair matched her complexion to perfection, being an exceptional burnished copper, a color that could not have come from any bottle or salon.

Aaron's gaze traveled further down her body to her breasts, which were covered by the thin t-shirt she had on. They looked firm, full, and ripe. He shifted her weight in his arms to try and ease the now painful erection. He had just been thinking about what color and how large her nipples might be. What they would taste like when he suckled them into his mouth? Her waist was small, but not the overly thin that most of the women nowadays were trying to achieve. Her hips flared out, and to his way of thinking, they were the perfect size for him to hold onto while slamming his cock deep inside her, giving them both pleasure for hours. Her jeans and the soft leather boots molded lovingly to her legs gave testimony of the length and muscle tone. She was any man's wet dream, and a vampire's worst nightmare rolled into one lovely woman. And he was very afraid this little slip of a human was what he feared more than anything in his entire fourteen hundred year existence. She was someone he had hoped never to meet.

Aaron was terrified that the woman who had begged for him to end her life was actually his life mate, and he was in no hurry to confirm that possibility.

There were several ways vampires knew their other half, their mate. Blood exchange was the most well known and quickest way to confirm what most of them knew. Sex, while the most enjoyable of the three ways, was also not the most reliable. The act of completion, during which both parties achieved release during intercourse, opened doorways to each other's minds through telepathy. An emotional bond was formed so tightly that one knew the feelings of the other at all times. Smell, the least reliable, was usually what lured the couple together. But when older vampires, and Aaron was one, got a strong aroma from their potential mate, it usually turned out they were the one meant for them. And Aaron knew as surely as he was sitting with her in his arms, she wouldn't be any happier about it than he was.

With a scent as powerful as Sara's, how could he possibly doubt that she was the one?

CHAPTER THREE

Aaron walked into the kitchen just as Duncan was closing one of the multitudes of cabinets. There were bags everywhere and more boxes than should have been necessary to hold groceries for one woman. All were marked with the logo of one of the local markets. He noticed a huge bowl of fruit on the tile counter. He picked up one of the oranges and put it to his nose.

The smell of citrus exploded in his senses. Feelings of sunshine and warmth on his skin, laughter ringing in his ears, and happiness moved through him. Memories. The wonderful memories of Christmas mornings as a child celebrating the season with his family.

He and his little sister would pour their meager stockings on the floor with the sounds of small toys, wooden and tin, clanking together as they rummaged for the small gifts. And at the toe, a single orange, a rare treat in both the season and their poor household.

"Has Miss Temple woken up yet, Duncan?" he asked as the emotions of the flashback receded.

"No, my lord, at least not for overly long. I do believe she has used the bathroom twice since her arrival. The monitor sounded when she entered that room earlier. I did find her on the bedroom floor near the bed just this morning, sir, and I put her back into it. However, the next time I went up, she was on the floor again, only across the room this time. I left her there. She must not have found any comfort in the big bed for some reason."

It would bother Duncan, Aaron thought, *that Sara was not in a proper bed. Knowing Duncan, he would probably purchase a new mattress if he believed that the old one had offended someone.* Aaron smiled at his dear friend.

"Maybe the bed is too soft for her wound. Have you gotten the food supplies I asked you to?"

Aaron knew that he could depend on Duncan; he had been doing that since they had rescued one another in the early eighteen hundreds. Both men starving, one for food, the other for blood, they had provided each other with what they needed most. Duncan had been his daywalker and protector since.

"Of course, my lord, you did ask me to."

Aaron felt his lips twitch at the look the man gave him. Prudently, he did not laugh at him. Duncan could be sensitive about such things.

"Yes, I know, but when was the last time food was brought into a household that you and I were living in?" While he did not feed from Duncan, a bond had formed between them in addition to a strong friendship. And because of it, Duncan would live, never aging for as long as Aaron did.

"I see your point. But I must say it was quite fun shopping for human food stuffs. I did not realize that things had changed so much in just one hundred years. And sire, you would not believe the variety of things. Why, there were several kinds of apples to choose from…I could hardly make up my mind. I did purchase plenty of fresh fruits for the young miss. Do you think she will enjoy them?"

"Duncan, I believe you need to get out more." Aaron sat in one of the new kitchen chairs that had been delivered the previous morning. "Yes, I do, even if she doesn't think she does. She'll need to eat well. She's much too thin as it is. Have you had any luck getting any help for the house? While I know that you are more than capable of getting everything done, with guests in the house, we don't want to give them the worry of thinking you won't be able to care for them."

"No, sir, I have not. It would seem that the previous master was quite the monster if you do not mind my saying so. No one will trust that you will not extract a payment of some sort to work here, as he did. And that you will not be as harsh or cruel as he."

Duncan was correct, he knew. It did not make the situation any better. That was why he had gone to see the Carlovettis. The young couple was well respected in both the human and the vampire world. He had gone to seek their help in bringing people around and convincing them to get to know him better.

"I feared as much," Aaron said sadly. "Hopefully, I'll be able to convince them that while I expect them to follow the rules set forth, I won't skin anyone alive who doesn't comply. I also plan to pay for the services rendered with a good wage."

Aaron had been doing a little research on the people he now commanded. They really were terrified of the leadership, and with good reason. In the month since he had become master, he'd only met with a handful of them, and they had been nearly overwhelmed with terror.

"I had heard that a 'skinning' was his minimum punishment for disobedience, and to do so while they lived...." Duncan shivered. "So it's true then, sire? You will have much to overcome, I fear." He said it as if he had fully expected him to accomplish it without any problems.

"I'm afraid so. And that was the minimum punishment. Once the little warrior wakes up, let me know immediately. She and I have a lot to talk about." He started to leave the room when Duncan stopped him by clearing his throat.

"My Lord...about the other guests, what should I do with them?" He suddenly looked nervous.

"They'll be here until we get this settled with Miss Temple. I don't want her to wake in a strange house with strange people." He could not resist a little teasing. "Are they proving too much for you, old man?"

Duncan huffed and walked away from him. Aaron laughed out loud. He could not wait for her to wake, he thought as he returned to his study. She was a distraction. A beautiful and stubborn distraction, one he wanted to kiss on the delicious mouth again.

~~~

Just before sunset, two days later, Sara woke up. Despite the great deal of pain from the bullet wound and soreness in a multitude of other places, she moved about enough to get herself going.

While sitting on the floor, she felt beyond the room, checking for others in the house, discovering the immensity of the building. She felt the presence of the Carlovettis and the vamp, plus one other person one floor below her — Duncan. She traced the others' faint signal to the lower regions of the mansion and realized they were both still at rest.

Moving slowly to the bathroom to clean up, she found her clothes, clean and neatly folded on the large sink. Her backpack sat on the counter, too, allowing her to brush her teeth first. This took a great deal of energy. As she sat down on the toilet, a knock sounded at the bathroom door.

"Yes?"

Duncan was standing just outside the open door to where she was. She didn't have much energy left, so she tilted her head slightly to look at him.

Duncan was not tall, but his slender stature made him appear taller. His skin tone was fair, his hair red and very curly, even as short as it was. Her first thought was Irish. It was his eyes that startled her the most. They were the deepest shade of green that she had ever seen. His smile at her made her realize that he had been talking to her all the while she had been studying him.

"Miss? It is I, Duncan. May I inquire if you need anything? I have been instructed to aide you in any way that you require."

Sara watched as he fussed with the stack of towels in his

arms.

"I was about to get into the shower. I'm pretty sure I can do that on my own, thanks. Unless you were told to help me with that too."

Sara had only planned to wash off and then sit down again. She suddenly felt...like something left uncovered in the fridge for too long.

For a full minute, he didn't say a word. His face, however, said it all. Shock, terror, and confusion flitted across his features as his face deepened in color, in embarrassment. She felt horrible about teasing him and decided to help him out and revise her statement.

"No, Mr. Duncan, I'm going to get into the shower. Alone. I'll be okay by myself. But thanks anyway."

"Very well, miss," he said with obvious relief in his voice. "Just pick up the phone and dial four if you need anything. Oh, and it's just Duncan, not Mr."

"All right, Duncan then. I'll be sure to let you know if I can think of anything. Thank you." He turned and looked at the bed. It was still made. She knew that he was wondering about it, but she didn't have the energy to explain she had not slept in a real bed for a long time. The hard floor was much more to her liking anyway.

Forty-five minutes later, Sara walked into the kitchen, startling Duncan. Also, there sat the man who had lied to her—the man from the hangar. *He is extremely handsome, this new master,* she thought again. *Arrogant as well, if the way he is looking at me is any indication of his personality.* That morning, he was dressed in much the same manner as he had been during their initial meeting at the hangar—black jeans, dark blue rather than black tee today, and tennis shoes, also black. *Why do they always dress like they are going to a funeral?* she mused, somewhat surprised that she had even noticed.

"Miss Temple, how are you this fine morning?" The humor

he wasn't trying to hide in his voice made him sound almost human.

"Fine enough to wanna smack that smirk right off your face," she told him. "And alive and kicking, no thanks to you either. You lied to me, bloodsucker." She looked around the brightly lit kitchen with its bright new appliances. Sunlight streamed through the open windows, letting sounds of the early birds and smell of fresh cut lawn in. "Shouldn't you be in your coffin somewhere or something? The sun is shining; I would think you'd be a crispy critter by now. I could help you along if you'd like. We could move outside to where the sun would make a more direct hit."

Sara was being snarky, she knew. She couldn't seem to help herself. She heard Duncan's sharp intake of breath. To be honest, she had forgotten that he was there. When Aaron threw back his head and roared with laughter, she turned to stare at him. *Christ,* she thought. His laugh went through her whole body, making her very aware of him as a man.

"Thank you, but no. Here is fine for now. As for the sunlight, I'm actually quite old. Therefore, I can stand the sunlight a little more than a younger vampire. As for you being alive, Miss Temple, I never said I'd take your life, only that I would end the one you were currently living. And I plan on doing just that, just as soon as you are able to get about."

Sara felt his look as if he had caressed her. It both excited her and made her angry. Anger she could handle. She wouldn't allow herself to think about the other right now.

"I won't become your blood du jour, bloodsucker," she snarled at him. *Yes,* she thought, *I do much better with anger.*

"Miss Temple!" Duncan barked at her. She felt herself flush with embarrassment.

"It's all right, Duncan. She's angry with me, as I am with her. So, we can get this over with now, Little Warrior. If you please, we can finish this in the dining room. Duncan has made you a wonderful breakfast, and you will need your strength back very soon." She backed up as he stood. His size did not frighten her. It was the man; he scared her in ways that she did not understand.

"No." She had to get away from him, away from all of them. *Now,* she thought, she needed to leave now.

"No? No, what, pray tell?" He took a step toward her. She was sure it was not to intimidate her, but it had. Slightly.

She looked at the door just behind Duncan. *I can make it,* she thought. "I want to be able to leave, please. I appreciate that you've seen to my wound since you are the cause of it anyway. I have a job, and my own place to stay, and...I'd like to go. I need to go." Hearing the panic in her voice, she hated it. Sara moved toward the door. She was not afraid of him, but rather of what he was making her feel.

"I caused your wound? However did you arrive at that conclusion?" he asked her as he wrapped his arms around his impressive chest.

Sara felt rather than saw him move. He had moved himself between her and the door, blocking her way. Damn it.

"You brought those men into the Carlovettis', didn't you? They were there because they wanted you dead." She was only half paying attention to what she was saying now.

The room had suddenly become an assault on her senses. His scent, deep earth and warmth, permeated the air. Then the smells coming from the kitchen itself. Bacon...God, when was the last time she had had bacon, eggs, toast, and sausage? Her stomach rumbled then. Hunger like she had never felt hit her. She lifted her eyes to his, wondering if he heard it too. But the look on his face made her forget all about the rumbling in her belly, and she centered completely on the man in front of her.

"You know why they were there? How did you get that information? Is this another one of your hidden talents? You seem to be just brimming with powers no one knew about, Little Warrior." He took another step toward her and then stopped when she retreated. She felt trapped.

"Of course. I'm surprised a big bad vamp like you didn't catch that. They were there to kill you and then blame it on the Carlovettis—an attempted murder gone wrong. Well, it did go wrong, but not like they'd planned, I guess. Now, if you don't mind, I'd like to be able to leave." This time, she tried to brush by him, but his voice stopped her cold.

"But I do mind, Sara Temple. You have a lot to answer for, and I plan on having you as a guest until I'm satisfied. Now, if you wouldn't mind going into the dining room while you break your fast, I will have a few of those answers now."

Compulsion—she had heard that vamps had this ability; she had used it herself when needed. With her blood loss and hunger, she could not fight him hard enough to break free. Little by little, she felt her resistance drain away until she was being led to the dining room. This time, he had won, but the next time...and she was suddenly sure that there would be lots more time spent with him...she would be the stronger of the two.

CHAPTER FOUR

Two hours later, Aaron was no closer to getting any answers from her than he had been when she had first come downstairs. She was by and far the most stubborn, frustrating woman he had ever encountered. It wasn't the fact that she didn't answer his questions that frustrated him; it was that she totally and completely ignored him. She shut him out as tightly as if he was not even in the room. Even threats didn't work, which should not have surprised him, seeing as to how she had asked him to end her life just a few days ago. He finally had to retire to the sublevels of his home. It wasn't that he was admitting defeat; rather, he could not take the highest point of the sun. But he warned her that he was not finished yet. And damn it all to hell, he had never gotten one whiff of her scent again.

At near sunset, Aaron went in search of Sara. He was going to get some answers from her or else...well, he would think about the "or else" later. He looked in the kitchen first and encountered Duncan, who seemed to be enjoying himself watching a cooking show on the small television on the counter.

"What are you doing?" He heard himself snarl at Duncan and felt horrible about it. Just as Aaron was about to apologize to him, Duncan answered.

"I thought if Miss Sara was going to be staying with us for a while, I'd learn to cook. It seems easy enough. What do you think she would like for dinner tonight? There are so many shows to watch from which I can learn different dishes."

Duncan was excited. Excited about cooking? For a human? Aaron decided that he would enroll him in cooking classes at the next opportunity. Then Aaron realized that his manservant had thrown him off track of his goal—finding Sara.

"I could care less. Where is she? I would have thought she'd be up and about by now. Terrorizing the world as we know it." *Okay,* he thought to himself, *now I'm being an ass.*

"I believe she is still abed, master. Oh, and Master Colin is here. He is below levels, I believe."

He only called him master when he was trying to make a point. But he was not in the mood to stay and figure out what it could be this time. Damn it, he was hungry and angry, not a good combination in most vamps. He wanted to find her. He turned on his heel and left the room. He was nearly up the stairs when he heard a small whimper.

Aaron flashed to the bedroom door where she was staying and found the door shut, but not locked. He walked in and found the bed empty, as was the room, but the sheets were covered in blood. Suddenly afraid, he strode to the bathroom door and knocked once. The whimper sounded again.

"Miss Temple—Sara, are you all right? Open the door this instant." He rattled the knob and knocked again.

"Go away." Her voice sounded weak. He tried to open a connection to her mentally. Physically, he could smell her blood. He was not sure, however, if it was from the bed or the bathroom. A sudden thought occurred to him. *Would she cut her own wrists?*

"Are you hurt? Well, of course, you're hurt, you've been shot. Do you need my assistance? Let me in to see to you. I'm telling you right now, young lady, you'd better not be bleeding to death in there. I'm going to be very pissed at you if you are."

He twisted the knob to no avail. He could unlock it on his own but preferred to wait and see how she would respond and what that revealed of her capabilities since that would reveal exactly what she was. Her powers were beyond what one would expect from a mere human being. "Open the damned door, Sara."

"What part of 'go away' did you not understand? Don't you people believe in privacy?" Even though she lowered her voice, he could still hear her mumble, "Stupid man. If I bleed to death, why should I care if he's pissed off or not?"

"I'm not going anywhere, damn it. If you don't tell me what's wrong with you, I'm going to break it down." He did not believe in all his life he had been more frustrated with anyone.

Just when he thought she was not going to answer, she said, "Isn't there some rule where you have to be invited in or something? I like that rule. It's a very smart rule when dealing with fruitcakes like you."

"It's my house, so it doesn't apply." He did not know whether to laugh or scream at her. "Are you going to answer me, or do I break the door down? I'll tell you now, Sara, it'll go better for you all around if you open the door. I'm not going to be very happy with you if I have to resort to busting my door down."

"First of all, why should I care if you bust in your own flippin' door? You'd have to pay for it, dumb ass. Secondly, I hurt. Why can't you just leave me alone? I just need to sit here for a little while to rest. Damn it, you are the most aggravating man I've ever...go away!"

He smiled. Damn, but she had a smart mouth. Tasty, too, he remembered.

"Hurt how, Sara? Let me in. I need to see you."

He heard a pleading tone in his voice because he realized he really did need to see her. He wasn't sure if it was because he wanted to strangle her or kiss her senseless. Either way, he needed the door open. He was getting the barest whiff of her now, the calla lilies and honey that seemed to be her smell to him. He drew in a deeper breath, opening his mouth so as to get the taste of her on his tongue. And despite his not wanting a mate, all he could think was, *mine.*

Aaron was nearly at the door-breaking point when he felt

a presence behind him. He turned and saw April, and she had Duncan with her. Neither looked very happy.

"My lord, what's the matter?" April asked him. There was a tone there. He could hear it but could not for the life of him understand it.

"Sara said she hurts. She won't open the door. Damn stubborn girl. She'd rather stay in there and hurt instead of letting someone help her. Are all women like this?" He turned toward the door again and hit it hard with his fist. "I won't have it, you hear me, Sara? I won't have it!"

"The whole house can hear you, you arrogant ass. I swear to...." She sobbed, and he felt it all the way into his soul. "Will you fucking go away? I just wanna sit here. Why are you doing this to me?"

Maybe, he thought, *if I piss her off enough, she will come out to me.*

"Me? I'm not doing anything. Yet, anyway. But as soon as I can, I'm gonna paddle your ass good. Now open this door."

He stepped back slightly and started to press his strength against the frame when April pecked him on the shoulder. He moved over to allow her to try. But paddling Sara's butt was sounding better and better all the time.

"Sara, honey, it's April. Will you open the door, please? You've worried us all quite enough."

"What's going on?" Demetrius asked as he, too, made his way into the room.

Just great, he thought, *now all they needed was —*

"Hello, everyone. Are we having a party up here then?" Colin Larimore, Aaron's best friend since the late nineteen hundreds, crowded into the room.

Aaron, still standing close to the door, heard her say, "For the love of St. Peter, is there, oh, I don't know, maybe a gardener or two who isn't in here we can bring in? I'm pretty sure that there are quite a few more people you can cram in this room to witness my ongoing humiliation. Why did I even get out of the stupid plane?"

Aaron laughed. He had not laughed this much in years. "No, everyone is here, love. Now, will you please open the door for us?"

Aaron could hear her moving around. Hopefully, she was coming to the door because he would not be able to stay still for much longer. He stepped back just as he heard the lock disengage.

"I didn't bring my clothes in, so all I have is a towel. I don't want any comments from you," he felt her whisper through his mind.

Every time she did that, he was surprised. The only time two people of his kind could communicate through mental communication was when they had exchanged blood or had sex. They had done neither...yet.

"I'll keep quiet, I promise. Now, open the door and come out here before I come in there and get you."

He hoped that it was a very large towel. He wasn't sure he could handle anything less than a thick comforter. The thought of what she may or may not have under the towel was making him hard. He did not want her to see him like this, especially with a room full of people. No, a small towel, or better yet, no towel, was better left to when they were alone.

When the door pulled open, there she stood. His breath caught, and he stilled. The towel was not big enough, he decided as soon as he saw all that creamy skin. She was beautiful, simply... *What the fuck?* he thought as he looked at her reflection in the mirror behind her and stepped closer to her. It was not the sight of her wrapped in one of his towels; God knew that alone was enough, but she had been beaten, and badly. Her back was covered in bruises from her neck to what he could see of her legs. When she turned and looked over her shoulder, their eyes caught in the mirror. He knew in that moment she realized he could see what she had been trying to hide. When she took one, then a second step back, he snapped.

"No. Don't move back. Turn around, Sara. Turn around and let me see." Anger made his voice hard, and he knew he was frightening her, but he could not help it.

"It's all right, really. That isn't what hurts. Not now, anyway. I'm fine, Aaron. I'll...I need to get dressed. If you would all just step...." She tried to step back and close the door in his face.

"Turn around, Sara. Now." He took another step toward her and felt his fangs drop in anger. His anger was turning him, his dark side was showing, and his beast was rising.

Aaron needed to make her understand it was not her he was angry at, but at the person who had done this to her. *Mine,* his mind screamed at him, and he wanted to hurt whoever was responsible.

Aaron growled to Duncan to get them out, all of them out. He, too, had caught the horrific details in the mirror, Aaron saw. As Duncan turned to usher the group away, he noticed April pale and Demetrius's own anger pulse through the room. It seemed everyone now knew the extent of her injuries.

"I'll not leave just yet, Duncan, old man. Something is going on, and I want to hang out for a bit. You understand?" Aaron heard Colin say to Duncan.

"Colin, go with Duncan, please. I'll deal with this. I'll explain when I come down shortly." Aaron did not take his eyes off Sara. She had backed all the way into the bathroom. Now she was standing against the far wall.

Aaron knew that Colin would not go far. During the seventeenth century, the two had become fast friends when a still human Colin had taken a beating for a young woman who had stolen bread for her small child. It had touched something human in the vampire's soul. Colin, near death, Aaron had offered him eternal life in exchange for him helping to serve and protect the then Master of the Realm, a respectable vampire by the name of Vlad de Moraes.

Aaron was beyond caring what anyone said or did now; all

he could think about was this badly beaten person in front of him and how much he needed to heal her, to touch her, and Christ, he needed to taste her.

"Duncan, I want you to call Thomas Reilly and have him get over here right now."

"Yes, My Lord. I'll call him immediately. Sire? Is there...I mean...." *Poor Duncan,* he thought. He was as lost as Aaron was.

"No, Duncan, I'll take care of her. Just call Thomas for me, please. Tell him to hurry." The door clicking closed resounded through the room.

"No, please, don't do this. I'm used to this. It's fine, really. I'm okay, much better, in fact. It's not what you think, honestly. I want to go. You can't make me stay. I need to go. I can't let him find me here. There's too much at stake. Just...I'm begging you to give me my clothes, and I'll go away. He'll kill you. Please?"

Aaron watched as tears streamed down her face. His first instinct was to let her go, anything to stop her crying. But he could not.

"I think someone has beaten you, love, that's what I think." He moved closer as he spoke until she cringed against the wall. "Sara, honey, turn around and let me see the extent of your injuries. I won't touch you, but I need to look at them."

She started shaking her head at him. "Okay, so it is what you think. Why? What can you do? Can you make the hurt go away? I want to go now. You have no rights over me, do you hear me? I want to go away from here."

She stiffened suddenly, and he jerked around to defend her. Anger boiled into the room from the man he'd forgotten about. Colin.

"Who will kill him? Aaron, what's going on?"

Aaron hid the grin that fought hard to turn into a laugh at the sight of Colin standing there. Colin was holding his broadsword in his hands, at the ready, in a pair of khaki shorts and an Ohio State Football t-shirt.

"Colin, please go with the others. I will explain in a moment. I can take care of this." At least Aaron hoped he could.

With a cool look toward the girl through the bathroom door, Colin left.

"And you aren't going anywhere. Not now. The doctor will be here soon, and then we are going to talk about this. Sara, I really need—"

"He will find out where I am again. I won't be able to protect her this time either if he does, don't you see? I can't let him hurt her again. I couldn't protect her before. It is imperative that I protect her at all costs. I cannot fail her again. Then there's the baby. Babies are all we have in the world, you know?"

While her babbling was disjointed, it wasn't very helpful either. He? He who? Baby? Christ, she was pregnant too?

"You're pregnant? Who is he? Your husband, is he the one who beat you? I'll kill the bastard." Some people, he decided, should not be allowed to live.

"What? No, I've never even had sex. No, April's baby. I want you to let me go." She was crying harder now.

Aaron would think about all she'd said later. For now, all he could think about was that she was hurting. He finally got her to come out of the bathroom with the promise that he would not make her bare herself to him. He went to his room to get her the softest shirt he owned for her to put on. She had explained to him how she had trouble pulling a shirt over her head, and that was when she realized just how much pain she was in. He helped her into the shirt, not looking at anything but her eyes. She managed to drop the towel only twice, leaving him with the briefest idea that the beatings had not been done only to her back and legs.

By the time Thomas got there, she was lying in the now clean bed and crying softly. Aaron stood at the door to the bedroom and waited, clenching and unclenching his fists. He could not remember being so angry in all of his considerable years. Nor had he ever felt so useless.

"Sara's hurting. I demand that you make it stop," he said in the way of a greeting.

"Can I see her first? It might make things easier that way."

Aaron could only glare at him. He had been Thomas's friend for two hundred years, but at that moment, he thought he might gladly stake him.

Aaron took a deep breath before he spoke again. "I would very much appreciate it if you could please examine her. Then I'd like for you to see if you can take away her pain. Please, Thomas. She's hurting."

Aaron felt Thomas's stare. Aaron could not imagine what he was thinking.

"All right," Thomas finally said. "Go downstairs, and I'll see what I can do."

"I'll be right out here. Yell if you need me or if she doesn't cooperate. She's...she can be stubborn at times," Aaron told him.

Aaron thought that was a bit of an understatement. She was frustratingly stubborn and infuriatingly obstinate.

As Aaron shut the door behind him, he heard Thomas say to Sara, "Come now, child, let's see what all the fuss is about."

CHAPTER FIVE

Aaron nervously paced the hallway just outside Sara's room, waiting for Doctor Thomas Reilly to bring him word of her condition. Aaron and Thomas had fought in the First Great War together and had become fast friends.

Nearly an hour had passed when the doctor stepped out of the room. He seemed upset and pale, even for a vampire.

"I have never seen anyone beaten that badly and remain conscious. That poor girl…that poor, poor girl."

They silently headed down the wide staircase toward the living room, where the others were awaiting word. As Aaron entered the room, everyone rose as one, concern in their eyes and faces. Aaron turned to Thomas and nodded, giving permission to explain the situation.

"I know without a doubt," Thomas said bluntly, "that Aaron did not cause this woman's pain. But someone has. According to the young lady, this is not the first time this has happened, nor will it be the last. I've given her something for the pain, so she's resting now. She has been beaten at least four times over the past two weeks, I would say. I can assume he's a large man, strong, and a mean son of a bitch by the bruising. This monster isn't only using his fists, although that's bad enough, but I believe he's using a bat as well. She said she has been thrown against a couple of walls too. She told me not to fuss overly much. I found this very curious, but she said that she heals initially very quickly. The bruising then takes the normal amount of healing time. This probably explains why there are only cracked ribs, rather than broken ones."

"Christ."

Aaron turned to look at Colin. He couldn't agree more.

"The young lady wouldn't tell me who it was, but I get the feeling she is terrified of him coming to the estate. Not for herself, but more so for you, Mrs. Carlovetti, and the other woman she needs to protect." Thomas paused slightly. "She seems to think you're pregnant."

Aaron looked at the new vamp and suddenly wondered if this was the babe Sara had been speaking of.

"Me? No, I'm not able to conceive. I've been converted for nearly a year now. She's mistaken. Vampires can't conceive. Can they?" April asked the room in general.

Aaron looked at the young vampire. Sara had killed the rogues to protect April, to protect her child.

"Actually, that's not true," Thomas explained to April. "It's rare, very rare, but it has happened. The woman is usually a new convert, pregnant or fertile just before the conversion. For it to be a whole year...I'm not sure. When was the last time, Aaron?"

But Aaron just could not wrap his mind around anything right now. "I don't know; about, oh, I'd say two hundred years or so."

"Yeah, that's about right. A simple test can tell if you are or not. And knowing her, or as little as we know, she probably can tell. That must be the child she was telling me that she had to protect. You're the reason she fought those rogues, to save you and the child you carry, I believe." Thomas looked concerned again. "She kept saying that when he found her, he'd hurt the child. You think it's the monster who did this to her?" Thomas looked around the room and his gaze settled on Aaron.

Sara said that she had not been able to protect the other child. Whose? he wondered. *And why would she feel the need to be responsible for someone else's child? Was it from the man who was now beating her, or someone else?* Instead of getting answers from her, the questions kept mounting.

"I take it she didn't tell you either," Aaron said, frustrated. "There are times when I think I should have drained her when she asked me to." He looked at April when she gasped. "I won't hurt her. I assure you of that."

"No, she didn't say who it might be, just that if he came for her, he'd hurt the babe. You think she's right then? Mrs. Carlovetti, why don't we do a test and see? Being older, Aaron can tell quicker than any test I can run if it's all right with your husband. He will just need to take a small taste of your blood, and he'll be able to tell immediately."

"This will be as good as place as any for you both to pledge your allegiance to me if you wish for my protection. I'm not requiring anyone to pledge to me just yet. I know the problems and issues that were a part of what you endured before. The blood exchange will leave me with the usual abilities, but I won't be able to summon you without your pledge." He wanted to make sure she was well informed before she agreed.

April looked to her husband. He nodded to her. "Yes. Yes, we've talked it over, and we will. I've never done this before. Will it...could it hurt the babe if I am pregnant?"

"No. I would never do that. I only need a drop."

She nodded.

Aaron stood and walked toward April. The allegiance had been around for as long as he had been a vampire. He also had pledged himself to several masters over the centuries. Most, of course, were dead. The few who had survived had released him from their bond long ago. They were still connected by blood; that could never be broken. As he had told April, they could no longer summon him to do their bidding.

April raised her unsteady wrist up for him to sip. He repeated the words of his vow to her. "I take your blood, April Carlovetti, as your pledge to me, who will become your master. You will be mine. I will, in return, pledge to you to keep you safe and protected for all my reign."

Aaron dropped his fangs and gently bit into her proffered wrist. He did not need much, either for the pledge or to see if she was pregnant. He looked down at the woman at his feet, then glanced over to her husband and said, "It would seem that I'm getting three for the price of two. Congratulations, you're about to become parents."

"Hot damn!"

With that, Demetrius picked up his wife and swung her around the room. He stopped suddenly, picked her up in his arms, and cradled her as if she was the most precious thing in the world. Aaron smiled in spite of himself.

Demetrius set his wife down on the sofa and knelt before his master. With tears in his eyes, he pledged himself to Aaron. He could do nothing but accept his oath as well.

~~~

When Sara awoke the next time, the room was completely dark, save for the moonlight spilling from the slightly opened curtain across the room. As was her habit, she reached out into the room and beyond to locate everyone and any hidden dangers to all within the household. She found the man responsible for her more immediate problems right there in the room with her.

"May I leave now?" she asked Aaron.

He completely ignored her question. "You'll be happy to know you were right about Mrs. Carlovetti. She is indeed, pregnant."

She knew that. That's why she had told him, the pompous ass. Well, screw it. If that was the way he wanted to be, she would no longer speak to him. He had not asked her anything, so she was not inclined to fill in the silence. She began to make her way into a sitting position. The plan was to go to the bathroom and get dressed and then leave.

After several minutes, he got out of his chair and walked

toward her and the bed. She continued to ignore him.

"Here, let me help you," he finally said.

She looked up at him. *Damned man. Does everything out of his mouth need to sound like a flippin' order?* "No. I have it under control. I'm hurt, not dead, thank you very much."

"You are by and far the most stubborn...I'm picking you up, prepare." And with that, he scooped her up into his arms.

"Put me down, you jackass. What are you doing? Do you want to break your back? Stop right now." Of course, he didn't, not that she really expected him to listen to her.

He settled her against the large counter in the bathroom and began unbuttoning her shirt. The taps to the large garden tub had been turned on before they entered, no doubt by some of his abilities, she thought. When he reached out and pulled a bottle of bubble bath off of the side of the tub and poured a generous amount into the spraying water, she snapped.

"You know I hate you...you...oh! Why are you doing this? I want to leave. Is it because you think I'll tell someone about you? I won't, not ever." She wiped angrily at her tears and turned to glare at him.

"Please don't cry, Sara. I know you won't. And if you learned to take proper care of yourself, this wouldn't be necessary. Now, Thomas — he was the attending doctor — said that you'd feel better after a long soak in the tub. We need to keep your wounds as dry as possible between soaks, though. Want me to help you get in?" He said this with a wolfish grin.

Sara looked at him for all of ten seconds. It was just too much. She gave him a hard mental push and watched as he flailed backward, ending up in the tub fully clothed, pink bubbles clinging to his dark hair and arms.

"Go soak yourself." And with that, she walked, hobbled really, back into the bedroom and out of the room. She heard him laugh as she slammed the door on her way out.

The man is insane, she thought, or she was. She had just

pushed a vampire three times her size into a tub. Stupid, she was just stupid.

~~~

By the time he had stripped out of his sodden clothes and dried himself, a good twenty minutes had passed. He was still chuckling to himself when he ventured into the hall with another towel knotted around his waist to go to his own bedchamber on the lower levels. There, he encountered Duncan. Aaron noticed that his assistant had an armload of his clothes with him. He smiled at the look on his face. *Poor Duncan,* he thought.

"Duncan, my man, just the person I need to see. Ah, I see my little warrior told you of my mishap. Good. Let me dress, and you tell me what she is up to now." He pulled the navy blue t-shirt over his head and dropped the towel on the floor. Next, he found the dark blue silk boxer briefs and slipped them on.

"Miss Sara said that she threw you into the tub, My Lord." Duncan stared at him with a look of total disbelief.

Next came the black jeans. Aaron was pulling them up over his lean hips as he answered him. His mouth twitched at Duncan's tone. Aaron had never heard him sound so disapproving before.

"That she did. That she did. I'll have to make her pay for that, I think. Tricky little thing, isn't she?" Aaron winked at the man. "Duncan, she didn't hurt me. It was my fault entirely, but let's not tell her that. All right?"

"People staying here without a proper house staff to care for them, a young human throwing you into a tub, you in her bed chamber.... My Lord, I do not know what to make of all this."

"Me either, Duncan, but I'm having the time of my life." Aaron handed the now sopping wet towel to him and bounded down the stairs in search of the woman who smelled like lilies and honey. He found her in the kitchen.

Sara was sitting at the large kitchen table, staring at something on a plate. She looked up at him when he entered the room. Her forehead was marred in what looked to him like confusion.

Aaron leaned over the plate and jerked back at the noxious odor coming from the congealed mass of red and white blobs on her plate.

"What's that? Smells...hmmm...different."

"Hush," she scolded him. "You'll hurt his feelings. He said he got the recipe off a cooking network. I think he said it was eggplant parmesan."

As he watched, she stabbed at it with a long-handled fork. He didn't think it was improving the look or the smell of it.

"Are you going to eat it?" he asked her incredulously.

She gave him a look, one he was coming to recognize from her as, *You are just too stupid to be alive, aren't you?*

"Of course, I am. I think so, anyway. What are you going to eat?" He could tell by the look on her face she realized too late what she had asked him. Warmth rushed through him, followed immediately by need, a need so profound he wanted to throw her on the table and feast on her, body and soul.

"Hmmm." He took a step toward her, only to come up short when she suddenly had one of her blades at his chest. "Are you offering yourself? Because there's nothing, I'd like more than to take a sip of you. Of you, your mouth, any part of you that you're willing to let me taste."

He moved his head toward her, toward her full mouth. He watched, mesmerized, as she licked her lips with the tip of her pink tongue. He groaned softly as he leaned closer to her mouth.

"Sara, I want to kiss you."

"No. You can't. I...I forbid you to try." Her voice was husky and soft.

Slowly, agonizingly slowly, he touched her ribs with his left hand, spreading his fingers wide along her. He brushed his mouth across hers in a small whisper of a touch. He encircled her other wrist with his right hand, pulled the blade from his chest, and stepped closer to her body.

"Sara...." As Aaron moved in for another light kiss, he cupped her breast in his hand and brushed his thumb across her nipple. He felt the warm flesh tighten and swell against his palm.

"I don't want this. You...stop right now. Stop...please, Aaron." Capturing her moan, her body arching against his, he dipped in again. This time. This time, she was his.

"Sara, let me taste you, love. Please?"

Before she could answer before he could taste her, she was pinned against the far cabinets, two feet off the ground by Colin, and Aaron was on the floor. Colin had his large bicep at her throat while working to take her knife from her hand. Aaron didn't think Colin would hurt Sara. He just wanted to disarm her. He saw her slam her wrists against his shoulder, and with a hiss of steel, twin blades came forward and into her hands. In a blink of an eye, everything changed from disarming her to her having a blade at Colin's heart with just enough pressure to draw a drop of blood.

"Colin, don't. She'll do it. Put her down. It's just a small... misunderstanding between us. Isn't it, Sara?" Aaron looked into her eyes.

"My Lord, this puny human cannot come in here and pull a blade on you." Anger and something hinging on incredulity was in his voice as if he couldn't believe Aaron would want him to stop protecting him.

Aaron ignored Colin for the moment and continued to stare at her. What he saw gave him pause; hurt, sorrow, sadness, bleakness, every depressing emotion you could imagine, but mostly he saw determination cross her face. She would kill Colin if, but only if, he gave her a reason.

"I have no doubt she is regretting it as we speak, aren't you, Sara? Sara, answer me."

Aaron stepped forward to pull Colin's arm from her neck and stopped. She pushed the blade into Colin's chest a little harder. Blood now dripped down his shirt.

She whispered through his mind, as she was unable to speak

with Colin cutting off her airway. *"I don't want to hurt him. But know that I will. I had a momentary lack of good judgment the other day, and I've decided I can't die just yet. You tell him to let me go, and I will stop trying to remove his heart."*

"Colin, she's very sorry for trying to kiss me just now. If you'd be so kind as to let her go, I might let her try again."

Aaron could almost feel her glare. It was so intense. He needed to make him let go, damn it. He was touching what Aaron considered his, and he did want to kiss her properly this time. But Colin's bark of laughter brought him up short.

"I will back off, little one if you would be so kind as to not unman me just yet. I may have something there that we can both enjoy later, if you'd like," Colin told her.

Colin and Sara both turned to look at Aaron as a feral growl emanated from him.

Colin lowered her very slowly. There was something, he would imagine, about having a very sharp knife at your dick that would make any reasonable man pay attention to details. Once she had both feet planted firmly on the floor, Colin stepped away from her. The next thing Aaron knew, she had flipped both Colin's feet out from under him. As he landed on his back with a whoosh, she was straddling his chest with her blades at a cross at his throat. *Shit*, he thought, *she's fast as well as dangerous.*

"I put you down as you asked, little one."

Colin put his hands up in surrender. Aaron decided not to interfere. If he pissed her off more, which he usually did, she might kill his friend out of spite.

"Yes, you did. You also opened my wound and made me bleed again vamp. I don't want to bleed anymore in this house, understand? I'm going to get off you, and you will lie very still until I am standing over there near the sink. If you don't comply, I'll have your master dead so fast, if you blink, you'll miss the show. Deal?" Colin nodded.

Sara moved off him and to the sink very slowly. Colin

watched her every move. So did Aaron. Once she was where she wanted to be, Colin got to his feet and bowed to her. She had just bested one of Aaron's best warriors, and Aaron had never been so relieved in his entire life.

CHAPTER SIX

Colin stared at the woman for nearly a full two minutes. She watched him as well. She never squirmed or gave any indication that she was frightened in any way. He was impressed with that. People, especially women, did not like to be stared at by such a large man; they began to think of ways to get as far away as possible when he did that.

It was not as if Colin was not a handsome man. He was, indeed. He had dark brown hair worn slightly long with two small braids down the left side of his face, which, if nothing else, gave testimony to his heritage. His eyes were as blue as the bonny sky that extended over his birthplace. He stood just over six feet, and while a large man at two hundred and fifty pounds, there was not an ounce of fat on him. Yes, he thought, this human deserved further study.

"Colin Larimore, I'd like you to meet Sara Temple. She is the warrior I was telling you about," Aaron told him.

Colin jerked his head around to Aaron, then back at the girl. "You took out six vampires?"

"No. There were seven if you count him and the Carlovettis. I took out three; he took out one," Sara told him as if it was nothing at all.

Colin looked back at his master and friend. "You didn't tell me she got more kills than you." Colin's opinion of the girl had just gone up several more notches. First, for killing three full vamps, and secondly, and most importantly, for saving Aaron.

"Shut up, Colin. I didn't tell you because it doesn't matter."

Colin grinned. He thought about pointing out that she was a mere human and he was a badass vamp, a master vamp at that, but reconsidered. That did not mean that he couldn't tease him about it later, he thought. And looking back at the girl, a woman, he guessed, he wasn't so sure she was completely human anyway.

Sara snorted. Both men looked at her. With a shrug, she started for the door out of the kitchen.

"Sweet bearded Jesus! You're bleeding! Shit! I didn't even smell it," Aaron yelled at her. Colin hadn't even noticed it himself until Aaron said something.

"That's because I didn't want you to. Why is this always a surprise to everyone? A house full of bloodsuckers, one bleeding human…do the math, and I bet you come to the same answer. I'm gonna find Duncan." This time, she was stopped by Aaron, who stood between her and the door out.

"I'll take care of your wound. Sit over there. Colin and I have some questions for you."

Colin raised a brow at his tone. "Bloody hell, Aaron, let the child get fixed up first." Colin was surprised at his attitude toward the girl. He had never heard him be so rude to a woman before. This was going to take some thought.

Sara turned to glare at Colin. When Duncan came into the kitchen a few minutes later, it was to find Sara and Aaron standing toe to toe screaming at one another. Colin thought it was the funniest thing that he had ever witnessed. Sara, in his estimation, was one or two up on his friend in zingers.

"I will not! You, sir, while an ass of major proportions are not my boss!" She shouted at Aaron, Colin thought, for about the fifth time.

"You will do as I say, right now, or so help me God, I will paddle that pretty butt of yours until you are begging me to give you an order."

Colin leaned over in his chair slightly to get a look at her pretty butt. *Yep—very pretty indeed.* He sat up when he heard Aaron growl at him.

"Are you even sane? Are you listening to yourself? Begging you for an order…oh my God, you are seriously delusional, did you know that? I have to get out of here before I need to be locked up right along with you." She was walking toward the door as she made this prediction.

Just as Colin started to watch her again, he noticed that Aaron was looking at him.

"Good heavens! What has happened now?" Duncan asked him when there was a lull in the noise.

"Well, let's see…he wants her to strip down to her bare skin, then let him tend to her, and she is taking exception to that. Actually, I think she's taking exception to a lot of things. But I think it's mostly to his tone. Or it could be his 'Godlike feelings about himself,' I believe is what she said." He laughed with Duncan.

"Colin!" Aaron snarled. "You are not helping. If you can't keep your opinions to yourself, then I'd prefer it if you'd leave the room."

"Yes, sire. I'll try to be good." Colin's look was one of pure innocence, but anyone who had known him for more than ten minutes knew that he did not have an innocent bone in his big body. And right now, he was having entirely too much fun to let Aaron's foul mood and temper bother him.

"I've had enough. Duncan, she is bleeding again, tend to her. Colin, don't let her out of your sight. I will be back in an hour." He looked directly at Sara and said, "I need to feed. When I return, we will have a talk, and I will get some answers." With that, he turned on his heel and left the big kitchen.

Sara promptly sat in one of the kitchen chairs and burst into tears. Colin could not blame her really; over the past several days, she had killed three men, been shot, dragged to a house owned by someone whom she did not know, nor did she want to, manhandled by him, and now she was bleeding again.

Colin looked to Duncan. He appeared to be ready to sit in the other chair and join her. Duncan didn't have a lot of experience with women, Colin knew. He would also bet that Duncan didn't have the slightest clue how to handle a crying one. When Duncan looked frantically at him, Colin sighed. *Oh well,* he thought, *no hope for it.*

"Come here, lassie. Let me see what all the fuss is about." He pulled her over to him, chair and all. He winced at the rough sound the chair legs made as he dragged them across the tiled floor.

"First I'm a child, now I'm a dog. You vampires sure have a way with women, don't you?" While she was no longer sobbing, fat tears were falling down her cheeks. He hated tears from a woman. They could turn him inside out faster than anything.

He murmured to her softly, not really saying anything while he inspected the bloody stain that now saturated her shirtfront. When he started to unbutton the shirt, which looked suspiciously like something Aaron would wear, she slapped his hands away.

"You gotta let me see this, sweetheart. Can you lift up your arm for me?"

When she tentatively lifted the front of the shirt up above the wound, he hissed. "Holy Mary, Mother of God, child, what's happened to you?"

"I was shot a few days ago. You just threw me against the wall. I've had a bad few days. I want to go to my own bed." She was crying again. Duncan set a large box of tissues in front of her, then busied himself with pulling out clean bandages, scissors, and tape. Colin nodded his thanks and continued with Sara.

"I donna think he's gonna let you go today, love. I'm sorry I hurt you, though. Did you really save Aaron's butt? Wish I could have seen that, I do." Colin tucked the shirt hem high into the pocket of her shirt to keep it out of his way while he worked.

Once Colin got the padding pulled away from her skin, he

was able to see the bullet wound. It was now just seeping blood instead of pouring, as it must have been doing earlier. He was shocked to his core that this woman was walking around as if nothing had happened. She had not made a noise when he had slammed her against the wall. She had, in fact, fought back. He had known grown men who would have been felled by less than this woman.

"You know, I could heal you right up with a couple sips of my blood…the bruises too if you'd like." He did not offer his vein often; seldom, if truth be told. She seemed to understand this without much acquaintance with him.

"No, but I thank you," she said demurely.

Colin found her politeness, bravery, and hardheadedness a huge turn-on and had had a semi-erection since he had held her against the cabinets. It had not gotten any better when she straddled him on the floor either. He made no move to touch her, however, other than to tend to her wound. Colin was aware somehow that she belonged to Aaron, even if he had not claimed her yet. The growls coming from his friend were too funny. Colin thought about how Aaron had spoken about her last evening when he called him to ask for his help.

Aaron had asked Colin to see if he could get a clue as to what "his little warrior" was or who she was. Colin doubted that she was fully human, but he was not getting anything from her as yet. He had not even been able to penetrate that considerable hold she had on her mind yet.

Duncan helped Colin get Sara put back together with fresh, clean bandages. Duncan also persuaded her to take a couple of pills to ease her pain a bit. Colin noticed the bruising around her backside. With a quick look at Duncan and with a small shake of his head, Colin decided that he would not ask her about it, but he would Aaron.

When Aaron arrived some twenty minutes later, he was in a much better frame of mind. Maybe not a better mood where

Sara was concerned, but that seemed to be the way with the two of them.

"What I'd like to know is, what are you, Sara?" Aaron asked without preamble as they adjourned to the living room. The Carlovettis joined them there.

Sara looked dumbfounded. "What do you mean, what am I? I'm a female, you dolt. I would have thought someone as old as you would have heard about the birds and the bees by now. Mr. Larimore, perhaps you could tell his dickship—oh sorry, I meant his lordship—the difference later."

"I know damn well and good that you're a female. That's not what I...shit." Colin watched his friend take several deep breaths before continuing. "You have the ability to cloak yourself against our kind, and you're a telepath. And just today, you threw me in the tub without touching me."

Colin burst out laughing. "You threw him in the tub? Oh, right and good. Wish I could have seen that. Did he make a pass, love? Ah, probably not. Yeah, love, I'll have a little talk with him about sex for you. Poor lad, I'd have thought...well, like you, I would have thought he knew his way around the female form."

Aaron turned on his longtime friend and growled, which to Colin's amazement, made him laugh all the harder. "Ah, Aaron, you canna begrudge me this? She's just a slip of a thing, and in the few hours I've been here, she has gotten the better of you several times."

"Sara has never gotten the better of me. I meant I slipped. And if you will remember, I think she got the better of you as well." Aaron was back to snarling again, Colin noticed, and he burst out laughing.

Colin had to leave the room. His mirth was such that he was afraid that if he had one more outburst, Aaron would truly kill him. Oh, but what a way to go.

~~~

"I don't know what you're talking about. As I have asked

several times now, I'd like to go. I have things to do. And believe it or not, they don't involve hanging out with you." She was beginning to hurt again. And damn it, she was hungry.

"Sit down. You aren't going anywhere, not until I have some answers." Aaron plopped down in the largest wingback chair she had ever seen and propped his feet up on the beautiful inlaid coffee table. *He fully expects to be completely obeyed,* she thought with amazement.

She looked to the Carlovettis.

"Mr. Carlovetti, do I still have a job with your airline?" She hated putting him on the spot, but without the job and a steady income, Mel wasn't going to be found.

"He isn't going to answer you. It's ultimately my decision who works for the people I protect. Now, sit your butt back down."

She ignored him and turned to look at April.

"Mrs. Carlovetti. Do I still have a job? I understand that you have to answer to...him. But I have to ultimately answer for myself." She gave Aaron what she hoped was a look of disdain, but she did not think it had the intended effect. He just laughed at her.

Sara stiffened in response, not from the laughter itself, but the feelings it stirred within her. She felt his laughter throughout her entire body. At that moment, she would have done anything to get him to do it again. It felt like a touch, a caress down her spine and through her core. She wanted him to pull her close, kiss her like he had in the kitchen, touch her breast, her nipple. She wanted,...no, she needed...him to touch her. The kiss in the kitchen had not been enough, not nearly so.

Putting everything she had within her to work, she immediately built a wall around her feelings, her emotions. If he knew how he had made her feel, she knew that she would never be able to leave this house again. And right now, she was not sure she wanted to.

Aaron crossed his arms over that massive chest of his and answered her. "You will be able to keep your job so long as I'm satisfied that you aren't a threat to what I'm here to protect. I have to make sure all the vampires in my realm are safe. I'm sure you understand."

She turned to glare at the man. If she had not staked him by morning, it would be a miracle, she thought.

"Like you protected them the other day? Like you made sure that Mrs. Carlovetti and her child were safe? You brought those men to them because you are so full of yourself that you couldn't go out without a guard." Her voice was calm and controlled, nothing like the turmoil running through her body. He brought out such emotions in her, most of which she did not completely understand.

She knew she had gone too far the moment he moved toward her. She turned to run from him. She only got as far as the door when he was on her. As before, instinct kicked in, and she fought back.

Just as he pushed her against the wall, she slammed down both wrists hard against the wall to arm herself. Twin blades were instantly in her hands, as before. As she swung the first blade in an arc toward his chest, he jumped back, narrowly missing having his gut sliced open. She marched him back, swinging the blades to and fro. Sara knew she could kill him with a single slice but could not make herself do anything more than back him away. He took a few nicks to his clothing, but nothing to cause him to lose blood.

Suddenly, out of nowhere, someone had her face down on the floor, a large weight holding her in place. Unless she could flip him off of her, she would not be going anywhere. Her head exploded with pain. Dizziness, then weakness slammed into her. Within seconds, blackness swam in her vision. She could feel herself sliding away, and there was nothing that she could do about it.

CHAPTER SEVEN

Colin lifted his body from Sara's, scanning her for injuries in much the same way she did when searching a room or other people. He assessed the extent of her injuries and was not happy to know that he had caused a concussion, and her wound, yet again, was open and bleeding.

"Shit! She's bleeding again. So is her head, Aaron. I'm afraid she has a pretty good concussion this time on top of everything else."

Colin rolled to his back. He was pretty sure that there would be hell to pay for this.

For the third time in as many days, Dr. Reilly was called in to have a look at the little human. And just as Colin had predicted, Thomas was royally pissed.

~~~

"You want to tell me why my patient is currently upstairs sporting a nice concussion, more cuts, and has had my stitches pulled out again?"

Aaron knew that Thomas would blame him. Of course, he was at fault, but still....

"Please, tell me that you didn't have anything to do with this, or so help me, God...." Thomas continued.

"Sara tried to attack me, and Colin only meant to get her away. He was protecting me." Aaron thought that this should be enough to make his point, but apparently, it was not.

"What, by running her down with a freight train? You do

realize she is mortal, don't you? Prone to damage from, oh let me see, everything sharp, hard, and fast? I don't believe this. I just don't fucking believe this. What the hell were you thinking? Or were you? You do have a brain in that thick skull of yours, don't you?" Thomas snarled at him.

Aaron was getting angry himself. He did not want her hurt any more than Thomas did. Aaron knew that he had provoked her into attacking him. He had been aggravating her in one way or another since she had walked into the hangar days ago. He just could not seem to help himself. It was either have her pissed off at him all the time, or he was going to throw her over his shoulder and take her to his lair. She affected him in ways he did not understand.

Sara had said that she'd had a...momentary lack of good judgment. Did she want to live now? If so, why? And most importantly, why now? Damn it, she was driving him crazier every day.

"If you keep this up, she...will...die. Is that the plan here? 'Cause if it is, just stop calling me in to patch her up again."

Aaron turned away from him and growled, "No, damn it, I don't want her to die. She needs to live. I think...she may...well, damn it. I can only smell her when she's unconscious, so I'm not sure yet. Damn stubborn girl." Turning back to his friend, his bewildered mind raced. "What the hell am I supposed to do with her, I ask you?"

Thomas stared in confusion. He waited for Aaron to continue. Then, suddenly, his eyes lit up with understanding.

"Holy shit, she's the one? She's your mate?" He started laughing. "Oh, this is too funny. You have yourself mated to a human who hates your guts."

Heat welled up in Aaron's veins. He tightened his fists. "I don't see what is so fucking funny about any of this. Do you think I want this to be happening just now...with her? She's human!"

Thomas stopped laughing and blurted, "What the hell does

that have to do with anything, I ask you?"

"I don't need this. What am I supposed to do with her if she is my mate? I have a whole realm to organize and make work. Do you have any idea what the last master did to the people here, what he took as his due as their leader?"

"Yes, I do," Thomas said somberly. "He was a horrible, sadistic man who should have been challenged years, if not centuries ago. As your mate, Aaron, she would be able to help you. Isn't that the way of our kind? Our mates are chosen to complement us, to be a 'mate' to us in all ways. What have you told her?"

"Nothing." Aaron turned away with a wave of disgust. "And I don't plan to either, not until I have some answers from her."

Thomas decided to stay the day within the mansion. Sunrise was very soon, and he wanted to be there to make sure that they left her alone for at least a few days, he told Aaron.

Later that night, Aaron was sitting in his office when there was a small knock at the door. He wanted to ignore it but was worried it might be about Sara. "Come in," he finally said.

"May I have a word, master?" April barely came across the threshold and would not look him in the eye.

"It's Aaron, April, please call me that. What can I do for you?" He motioned for her to have a seat in the chair across from his messy desk.

He had inherited the mess on it and the one in his realm when he had killed Carlos. He had not thought of either for several hours now.

"I'd like to know what you plan to do with my friend, Sara."

Aaron was surprised by the question, but more so by her tone. The timid woman was suddenly gone, and in her place was a fierce protector. He wondered if she even realized it.

"What do you mean, 'do with her?' I think I've made my position very clear on this; she will give us the answers we need to ensure our safety." He smiled to himself when she flushed slightly.

"I would like for you to let her go as soon as she is able to be on her own. I want her to go back to work for us and not be bothered again. She has gone through a great deal in the past few days, saving your life notwithstanding. If you would like, I'll take full responsibility for any and all actions in the future. I just want her to be safe." April was begging for Sara's life, he realized. She thought he was going to kill her.

Aaron leaned back in his chair. He had been sitting at his desk for nearly an hour just thinking about the girl upstairs. It had been two days since she had been hurt again, and according to Duncan, who checked on her nearly every hour, she had not moved once. He himself had been in to check on her several times a night just sitting in the big-armed chair next to the bed, and was more than a little worried. Not about her—no, Thomas was a good doctor. He was worried about what she would do when she found out he was her mate.

"I don't think I can do that, April. She knows a great deal about us. She can do a great many things that haven't been explained. I appreciate you wanting your friend safe, but you must also understand my position in this."

Her being my mate notwithstanding, he thought.

"Sara knew all this and a great deal more before she saved our lives." She pointed out to him.

"True, but we didn't know that then. She has made herself known to our kind now, April. She killed several of our kind. I realized why she did it. I do. But what if she were to...?" He stopped when she suddenly stood.

"No! All that would have made it much easier to kill any of us had that been her intentions. You must agree that had she wanted us dead, she could have just let those rogues take us out or saved Demi and me and let them kill you. But she didn't. She saved your life in addition to ours and my child," she snapped at him. She then stormed out of his office, slamming the large oak door with a resounding bang.

Later that night, as he had for the past several nights, he stood over the bed looking down at his mate. He wanted to lie down beside her and hold her close to his body. He wanted to be beside her, inside of her. He wanted her with a near tangible intensity. But there was too much unknown between them for that to happen. He had no choice — he had to let her go, but he would keep an eye on her.

CHAPTER EIGHT

Sara woke the next morning. Her body ached…in fact, she did not believe that there was one inch on her that did not hurt in some way. She wanted to get up…needed to really but did not have the strength to do it, so she had little choice but to ring downstairs and ask for help. Picking up the dark blue phone on the table next to the bed, she pressed four for Duncan. He answered on the first ring.

"Good morning, miss," he answered in the way of a greeting. She smiled at his obvious chipper tone.

"Mr. Duncan, I was wondering if you could help me to the bathroom. You don't have to come up now if you're busy. Just, you know, whenever you have the time." She hoped it was soon, as she really had to pee.

"I'll be right up. Can I bring you something? Dr. Thomas said that you can only have liquids for now. How about some nice tea or some broth, maybe?" There was so much hope in his voice, but she so did not want to think about anything liquid right now.

"Maybe later, after…I think after my shower. I like tea." She liked iced tea without sugar but did not want to think about that either.

Within two minutes, Aaron was knocking at her door. When she told him to come in, he opened the big door and went right to the bed beside her.

"What are you doing in here? Where's Duncan? He said he was coming up." He, of course, ignored her questions.

"Let me see if I can get you something to wear first. There should be a robe hanging—ah, here it is. Can you stand at all, Sara? There's a good girl, up we go." If she did not need to use the bathroom so badly, she would have just stayed where she was.

Aaron was very careful with her, for which Sara was grateful. She felt the pull on the stitches again and was careful how she moved. Once she was completely upright, she stood for several seconds until the room stopped spinning before she moved on.

Sara looked up into his eyes. Aaron was an incredibly handsome man, and when he smiled, like he was doing right now, her heart kicked up a notch, and her body responded like it was starved for him—some part of him.

"If you keep looking at me like that, I'm going to finish what we started in the kitchen, Sara." He moved his mouth closer to hers, just close enough that she could feel his warm breath gently move across her skin. "I want to kiss you right now, taste you, but I fear that I won't be able to stop once I start."

"Why?" She was unsure if she was asking him why he wanted to kiss her or why he couldn't stop once he started.

Aaron did not answer but pulled back from her just as Duncan came into the room. She did not look at the other man. All she could focus on was how suddenly hungry she was for a taste of him as well.

"Duncan, could you please see that our guest gets to the bathroom? I have...other business that requires my attention."

"Of course, My Lord. You can depend on me."

Aaron left the room as soon as he handed Sara off to the very capable Duncan. He turned to look at her before stepping into the hall. She felt him whisper through her mind.

"We aren't finished, you and I. I want you, Sara. I want you with a desperation I've never felt before. And I can feel you want me as well, smell your need on your body when I'm near you. And I intend to sample that very lovely mouth and so much more of you when you're

better. Count on it." Then he swept out of the room, leaving her dizzy with a need for him to do just what he said.

Sara tried not to lean too heavily on Duncan, but she was still very weak. They didn't make any record breaking time getting there, but she was in one piece when they got to the sink. She assured him that she would be fine for the next few minutes and closed the door on him. She could tell he did not want to leave her alone, but he could see the wisdom in letting her have her privacy. While she was attending to herself, she could hear him fussing around on the other side of the door.

Sara looked into the huge mirror over the sink after going to the bathroom. Her face was bruised, but not overly so. The mark on her neck where Colin had held her against the cabinets was now several shades of browns and blues. Her hair was a mess, and reaching for the comb on the sink, she tried to straighten it as best she could but simply did not have the energy.

Aaron…Mr. MacManus…had started to kiss her twice now… once in the kitchen and then just now. Why? she wondered, then flushed. She was not so much concerned with why he wanted to kiss her, she realized, but that he had not.

When she finally opened the door, opting wisely, she thought, not to take a shower, Duncan stepped quickly to her.

"Too much, I'm guessing; back to bed with you." He put his shoulder under her good side to gently guide her to the bed. He had made it, she saw, stripping off all the linens and putting on fresh sheets. He had also folded back the gorgeous quilt so that she could get into it with ease.

She had only taken two steps when he stopped her. Without a word, he gently picked her up into his arms and laid her back on the bed. She was exhausted and hurting and did not utter a single protest when he lifted her. Then he fussed the blankets around her, fluffing her pillows behind her head.

"Now, I think you need to eat something light. I will go down and brew you up some tea with honey, and maybe a little broth…

beef, I think. Dr. Thomas left instructions on how to make both, and to be honest, I've been practicing while you slept. I think I've about got it. What do you say?" He winked at her, and despite how badly she felt, she laughed.

"Oh, Duncan, where have you been all my life? Thank you, I'll take the broth and tea now, please."

Sara really just wanted to go back to sleep, the walk to the bathroom having taken a great deal out of her. She also knew that she needed to rebuild her strength if she stood any chance of leaving this house before she became someone's lunch. She was not going to ask again if she could leave, she decided. It was time she left, and if she had to hurt a certain arrogant ass of a vamp to do it, then she would.

Sara must have dozed off. Duncan was about to turn and go back downstairs when she stopped him.

"Duncan, I'm awake now. Please, come in. That smells wonderful." She tried to sit up a little straighter, but it required too much effort. She almost laughed at the expression on his face.

"How are you feeling, miss? You look a little...well, if you don't mind my saying so, miss, you look like something that has been run over a few times."

"Better than I look, I guess. It has been a rough couple of days. Do I really look as badly as I feel? No, don't answer that. I'm feeling better, thank you for asking." Somehow, she knew he was not trying to be funny but simply did not get the slang. He was always so proper. She wondered what he had been before he had started working for Aaron.

"Yes, it has. Here you go. You eat as much as you can, please." He put the tray across her lap, and as he turned to go, she asked him not to leave just yet.

"Please, Mr. Duncan, if you wouldn't mind keeping me company for a little bit. I won't fall asleep in my soup if you stay."

Duncan sat in the chair that faced the bed. He then reached into his inside jacket pocket and pulled several golden-colored spoons from his left pocket and then a white cloth from the right. He then proceeded to polish them.

"What day is it?" she asked after several minutes of eating. The meaty, rich broth was very good. It was warm and delicious going down. The tea was too sweet, but she drank it as well.

"Wednesday, I believe, miss."

He was putting the spoons, which she was sure were real gold, back into his pocket. She watched in astonishment when he reached into his front jacket pocket and pulled out another small cloth bag with several knives of the same golden hue and design. He looked up at her curiously as he began to polish them as well.

"No, I mean the date? I know it's mid-June, but what's the actual date?" *Gee,* she thought, *it has been a rough few days if I can't even remember the date.*

"Oh, it's the sixteenth," he said.

"Oh no, I need to go into town today. I have to mail something, a payment. I should have mailed it three days ago. It'll be late for sure." As she made to get up, alarmed, Duncan moved to settle her back into the bed.

"I don't believe it would be wise of you, Miss Sara. You won't be able to go anywhere today. You can barely walk; going into town is out of the question. Here, lie back down." Once he got her back in bed, he sat back in the chair. "I'll do what you need done, so don't you fret. Just tell me what you need, and I'll see to it as soon as you've eaten."

"I can't ask you to do that. You're not here to serve me, and I need to go soon anyway. If you're afraid, I will come right back, so the bloodsucker doesn't have to know. I wouldn't do anything that would get you into trouble, Duncan." She liked the gentleman too much for that.

"Nonsense, the bloodsuck...I mean, his lordship will know because I will have to tell him that I allowed you to leave. Tell me what needs to be done. His lordship would want me to ensure that you are well taken care of."

Sara looked at him, and through his mind, searching for a reason a stranger would help her; when she could find no other motive than a desire to simply help her, she sighed. She doubted that his lordship would give two figs whether she was taken care of or not. The money needed to go out, though; someone depended on her to make sure the bills were paid.

"I have to have my backpack…could you get it for me, please? You don't know how much I appreciate this, Duncan."

After Duncan retrieved it for her, she opened the larger part of it and pulled out all her personal stuff. She always carried extra things with her; clothes, two pairs of pants, three shirts, several pairs of lacey panties, a couple of bras, socks, and a windbreaker. Also in her bag were a wallet, brush, toothbrush, hair barrettes, and ponytail holders. There was also a small bag that held her personal feminine things and a large zippered pack that was full of stationery. This, she laid aside. When she reached inside again, she pulled out a large stack of cash. Sara put everything back into her bag and was writing out an envelope while she explained what she needed him to do.

"Please, get a money order for eight hundred twenty-five dollars and put it in this envelope and mail it at the post office." She hoped again that she was doing the right thing, but she did not really have a choice. "Here is some extra money for special delivery. Hopefully, this will cover it. I don't have to mail the money this way very often, so I'm not sure how much it costs."

Sara had less than twenty-five dollars left in her hand when she was done counting out the money for him to mail. If she was not able to go back to work soon, she'd have to figure something else out quickly.

"Thank you, Mr. Duncan. You don't know how much I appreciate this. I'm not used to…having people help me isn't something I've ever…. Thank you."

"You're very welcome, miss. It's always a pleasure when a man can help out a damsel in distress." He winked at her as he put the envelope and cash into his jacket pocket with the golden spoons.

And with that, he gathered up the tray and left her to her nap. She was nearly asleep when he was closing the door behind him.

CHAPTER NINE

"Well, I think you are about ready to be discharged, young lady. How does that sound?" It had been a long week, and she was feeling tremendously better. And Thomas Reilly was finally letting her go home.

"Perfect, sir." She needed to get this over with now. "I'd like to know if I can make arrangements to pay you. I don't have much money. I'll be able to pay you when I have a more steady income." She felt herself flush.

"Miss, you don't owe me anything. I'm...Aaron is my master, yes, but he's also my friend. I came here to take care of you, of course, but the opportunity to aggravate him is a bonus all by itself. So don't worry your pretty little head about it. However, if you find the chance when I'm around to give it to him good, then I'll consider that a gift." He grinned at her as he stood to leave. "Now that that unpleasant business is taken care of, Aaron said you are to be taken home as soon as you're ready. I don't think he's all that happy about you leaving, and I wouldn't be too surprised if he were to pop up now and again if I were you. Just to check on you, so to speak. You are just to let Duncan know, and he will be happy to take you there."

There was more to it than what he was actually telling her, or trying not to tell her, she was sure, but she was just too excited to care about it right then.

Sara had not seen Aaron all week. She did not know where he was or what he was up to, and she had never asked. Duncan or one of the others came to see her every day, more so now that she could get out of the bed and even more since she could move around. But she had never left the room, not wanting to confront the master of the house.

She gathered up her meager belongings and was ready to leave some thirty minutes later. She found Duncan in the kitchen again and asked if he was ready to go.

"Yes, miss, all ready when you are. I'm sorry the master could not be here to see you off, but he has been…well, he has been…what I mean to say is that…." he started to say. She didn't need him to make excuses for his boss.

"It's all right, Duncan. I'm more than ready to get out of here. I have lots of stuff to do, as I'm sure you do. You've been great, but I really need to get away from him. I do have a thank you note for him if you could see that he gets it." She handed him one of her envelopes of a pretty shade of blue.

"Oh no, miss, it isn't like that at all. He's new to this realm, and there are so many details to see to. The area and household were left in such horrible shape for so many years. The previous master was such a tyrant and a sadist. His lordship is trying to get the other vampires to come to him with their needs. He so wants to help them, you see."

Sara nodded at him in the way of an answer as she turned away. She had not known Aaron long, but from what Duncan had told her sounded like something he would do.

Sara had Duncan take her to the Carlovetti Airlines hangar. The private airstrip was just outside of Zanesville, about fifty miles from Columbus and the Columbus Airport. Carlovetti Airlines did an amazing amount of business, taking commuters to and from larger cities like New York and Chicago.

Sara's van was just where she had parked it nine days ago when she had first met Aaron and saved his life. She was grateful it was late, and everyone had already gone home. It gave her a few minutes to resettle herself and clean up in the hangar before leaving. She did not think it wise to bathe in the little creek nearby to where she parked tonight. Her wounds were still healing, and she did not think the dirty water would be very wise for her health.

It was not as though she didn't want Duncan to know where she lived. It was how she lived that she was keeping secret from him and everyone else. She was sure that she would never have been able to leave the big house had they known that she lived in her van and had been for several years now. When it got cold enough that blankets did not keep her warm at night, she moved into the local YWCA for a few months. When spring broke, however, she moved back. After she had taken a quick shower, she drove to her usual place in the middle of the wildlife preserve near the airstrip.

When she was sure that it was safe, she pulled out the rest of her savings. With the money left over from her recent payment out to Sunny Side Up in Nevada, she had nine hundred and forty dollars left until her first check again. If she were careful and ate sparingly, she had just enough for another payment. That was, barring any unforeseen accidents, and lately, that was becoming too much of a habit.

Sara had been very grateful that the Carlovettis were going to use her as a "daywalker." She would be answering the phones and making flight plans for the other pilots until she was released to fly by Dr. Thomas. She was okay with the forced confinement. The everyday movement on the tender wound could cause her problems at fifty thousand feet that she did not want to chance.

Sara put everything away and sat down to focus. She had to be careful when contacting her friend Mel by telepathic means. Mel was an extremely important part of the magic Sara and everyone else used in the world. Mel was magic; actually, her full title was Queen, Mistress of Light, Keeper of All Magic. She was responsible for all the good and bad magic in the world. Her goal was keeping the world safe from the ones who would abuse the power and thus destroy the earth as humans knew it.

Sara had met Melody about fifteen years before. The queen had been looking for guards to beef up her security, as she was to take a mate soon. Marcus, her personal guard, had suggested she come to a training facility to watch the young girl fight.

The training facility had been the Molavonta Kingdom guard's idea. They had suggested that Mel look into the human sphere and see if there were any there who could be trained. The facility had been charged with a magical beacon to attract those humans who may have special abilities that went beyond sword and gunplay. There was a watcher, or guard, at each place to keep track of all who entered.

Sara had been young, very young by any standards, but she fought like the warrior that Aaron continued to call her. Her magic was strong, even untouched and without much training. She bested man after man with the strength and style that was unique to her. Her ability to memorize each stance, each move immediately gave her a step up in the learning curve and made her stand out as someone to be reckoned with.

The swords used to train with were much too heavy for her at eleven years old, being too long and cumbersome. Mel had some blades, the ones Sara still used today, fashioned for her by her own blacksmith. The steel was stronger than anything made in this world and had anyone taken a closer look, they would have seen the markings, charms for safety and wellbeing crafted right into the silver. Those alone made the weapons stand out from anything human-made. Several weeks after their first meeting, at the age of twelve, Sara Temple became the youngest guard of the queen ever taken into service

"Hello, Little Warrior, how goes it? It has been a while," Mel said as soon as the pathway was open.

"Yes, I have been detained. And I'd appreciate it if you'd stay out of my memories." The pathway between the two women had always been strong. Sara had never tried to block Mel from her mind, but

some things, like her memories, were off-limits.

"*Yes, so I've seen. How is your vamp, love? Is he getting you all hot and bothered still?*"

"*Stop that. He's not my anything. You are well, my queen?*" She was not going to think about the fact that he had almost kissed her.

"*He still searches for me, Sara. And it is only a matter of time before I must face him again.*" Sara knew she was right.

Sherman, Mel's mate, had found Sara recently and had nearly killed her, demanding information about where she had taken Mel. She could not fight him back, nor could she defend herself against him. It was a part of his magic as an immortal and Mel's mate.

"*Yes, he does, but he won't find you. I promise you this. You are hidden away from everyone, especially him.*" That was the one thing she had done right, not letting anyone know where she had taken Mel.

"*I wish to see you. Come to me soon. I miss you very much. And, Sara, it has come time for us to talk. We have a great deal to talk about.*"

Sara could probably simply fly out in one of the little Cessnas, but she would have to file a flight plan, and that would leave a paper trail that neither she nor Mel could afford. And why all of a sudden, did everyone seemed to want to talk? She liked things the way they were before when she would go days on end without having to have a conversation with anyone except for the controller on the ground.

"*I need some money first. I've had to spend nearly all I have in order to pay the monthly accommodation costs where you are. I will need at least a month to recoup my funds. Can you wait that long?*"

"*I wish you would go to the repository and get what you need. There is plenty there for you to use as you see fit—jewels, cash, and gold. You should be getting paid for what you are doing for me, what you are doing for all mankind. Soon, Sara, all will be well, and I will remember all that you have done for me.*" Sara could feel herself blush at her praise. They were not even in the same state, and she could embarrass her.

"You know that I can't do that," Sara told her. *"How would I explain the need for funding to keep the queen hidden and not have several hundred of your subjects hounding me for details on where you were, why you were there, and why weren't you home with them? Besides, you know as well as I do, there's still a warrant out for my immediate death. Even if I could get the funding, dear Shermie would use that as a means to find me, then, through me, you."*

"You're right, damn it."

~~~

Sara had never let Mel know to what extent she had gone to keep her safe. But Mel knew like she knew everything that Sara had gone through.

Sara had been on patrol when Melody had been injured four years ago during the blast that rocked the castle in the kingdom of Molavonta. Sherman had somehow gotten Mel to go to the lower levels where he had drugged her. He had then put her into a cell that had been warded and charmed with black magic. In her weakened state, she could not fight against him and his magic. The explosion was set to go off in the early hours of the evening when everyone was having dinner in the main hall. Mel had reached telepathically for anyone to help her. Luckily, Sara had been the one to hear her. Ten minutes before the bomb went off, Sara reached the cell and began to remove the wards to get her out. The bomb went off, killing six guards and twenty members of the royal staff. Sara had just managed to drag Mel out of the building and into an open field where she delivered Mel's stillborn child. Moving Mel through a maze of ports into the human world, she settled her in Reno. By then, Mel was so weak and close to the fade of her life that Sara put her into a coma-like state until she could recuperate. Royalty like Melody were true immortals, never dying. When they tired of life or needed an extended rest, they changed themselves into something magical.

Mel's mother, Savannah, was a fairy ring somewhere in a little town outside of Dunbar, Ireland.

A warrant was issued for Sara's immediate death, as well as a separate warrant against the six guards that had died in the explosion. The council had thought the six men, though dead, had been helping Sara remove the queen from the castle, and a slight miscalculation in timing had caught them unawares. The warrant, when served against Sara, would then be issued to the guards' families, and they would be held accountable in lieu of men's lives. Until Mel, her mother, or grandmother could be found, Sherman was running Molavonta. He could not control the magic, but the castle had become his playground.

The staff at the nursing home, Sunny Side Up, had no idea who or what their charge was. Sara had been able to cast her into the shape of a very old man who would require constant care. With the help of a small mental push from Sara, the staff gave the nice old man the best possible care, above and beyond anyone else that was there. She made sure that all of the other residents at the home received good care as well. That way, no one was the wiser about the care being given to one special needs patient.

"You will reign again soon, and then things will be better for us all," Sara vowed.

The old friends talked for a few more minutes and closed the gap. They could not use their magic for long, or it could be traced to its source and destroyed.

~~~

Mel lay in her bed, thinking about Sara long after she felt the girl fall asleep. Mel had begun working her magic throughout the world in little increments so as not to cause a trail back to the nursing home since she woke two years ago. She was getting much stronger every day and would very soon need to face her mate. Sara had given up so much to protect her when everyone else had given up the search for her.

Mel was sending more and more power to the young guard

whenever she could manage it, siphoning off some of hers to strengthen Sara's power base. This was part of what she needed to talk to Sara about as soon as possible, as she needed to find someone to take her place soon. Sara knew nothing about the added powers and would be magically stronger than any living human very shortly.

As a now unmated queen, Mel could have no more children. A royal-born queen could only conceive once. This was another reason her talk with Sara needed to be soon. Maybe Sara's vampire would be the one to help them both. Melody, Mistress of Light, Keeper of All Magic, had a lot to do before her friend came to see her.

CHAPTER TEN

"Carlovetti Airways, how may I help you?" the voice at the other end of his phone asked, and Aaron took a deep breath.

Aaron had been both dreading and looking forward to calling Sara all day. Now that he had her on the phone, his mind completely shut down. He glanced down at the index cards full of notes that April had helped him with yesterday. The first card said, "Ask about her health."

"Hello, Sara, how are you feeling this fine evening?" His hearing was excellent, so when she muttered, "Well, hell, fuck a duck and watch it waddle," he nearly laughed out loud. He was glad her disposition had not changed at least.

"Mr. MacManus, the Carlovettis are not here yet. I'll be sure to tell them you called." He was sure she was about to hang up when he stopped her.

"I called to talk to you, my dear. You didn't answer my question. How are you feeling? Better, I hope."

"I'm fine, sir." Her tone was cool, almost distant. But he knew she was far from indifferent to him.

He caught himself wadding up his notes and stopped. As he was smoothing them out, he flipped to number two. *Very funny*, he thought. "Breathe, and don't fuck this up," it said. He would have to tell April how helpful her notes were the next time he saw her.

"I need for you to do something for me...well, me and the Carlovettis, that is. I need you to help me out on Friday night."

Sara did not acknowledge Aaron in any way. He knew she was there; he could hear her breathing. "Sara?"

"Yes, sir?" He had never known anyone, human or vampire, that could convey so much in two little words...frustration, aggravation, irritation.

"Did you hear me?" he asked again. "I need a favor; we need a favor from you."

"I heard you. Believe it or not, I hear perfectly well. I'm really busy here. You've stated your business. I need to go."

He had been anticipating this since Monday, how to ask for her help by writing notes, practicing, but this was going nothing like he'd planned. Why did she have to be so damned stubborn all the time? April said that Sara wouldn't say anything unless he asked her a precise, direct question. He would have to resort to his damned notes again.

"I was wondering if you'd be my date this Friday night at the Alliance Dinner at six-thirty? It's here at the mansion." He wondered if he sounded rushed and didn't think so.

"No."

Nope, not going well at all. She was not supposed to flat out refuse. Notes, he had to keep with his notes. He felt like he was in high school kid on his first date and that he had had his big sister write out what to say.

"Let me explain this better for you. The Alliance Dinner is for every vampire in my realm to come here and pledge their fidelity to me. All are required to attend, including the Carlovettis. In addition to them would be the person or people who made an attempt on our lives a few weeks ago. I want you to be there to help keep an eye on everyone dear to us both. So let me ask you again, I was wondering if you'd be my date this Friday night at the Alliance Dinner at six-thirty?"

For a long, tense moment, she did not make a sound. There was such a delay in her response, in fact, that he had thought she had hung up. "I don't really have a choice, do I?"

Aaron felt like hell now. She could make him madder than all hell one minute and then make him feel like the worst kind of heel the next. *Damn it*, he thought as he stretched out his shoulders.

"Yes, you do, Sara. You can say no. You're actually quite good at it. You certainly say it often enough to me. Anyway, just say no, and that will be the end of it. Is that what you want?"

"Thank you, Mr. MacManus, but I don't really. You and I both know that. Is there anything else, sir?"

"No, I'll work out the details on what I need from you, and then I'll call you sometime in the morning."

"Yes, sir," she said shortly.

"Oh, and Sara, it will be important that you call me by my first name if we are going to be seen as a couple. It's Aaron, not Mr. MacManus."

"Yes, sir." Her temper was rising. He could tell by the venom she put into her answer now. He grinned. How he hoped she would put as much passion into making love as she did her answers to him.

Long after he hung up, he thought about what he had done to her. He realized he really had made it so that she had no choice in the matter; he knew that when he had worded it the way he had. But damn it, he wanted to see her, needed to see her. If this was what it was like to have a mate, then to hell with it, he thought. It was not worth the damn problems she always seemed to cause. Then he smiled. He was going to get to see her again soon.

~~~

Now, she thought, I need to get a dress. Not just any dress either, a classy one. She knew that this was a formal affair because she had heard April telling her husband about the dress she had picked out. The alterations alone cost more than Sara made in a week. How she was going to afford a dress for this thing was beyond her.

Sara wasn't used to asking for help, so it did not occur to her to ask for it now. In the end, she found herself at the mall looking for a suitable, affordable dress at every boutique and store there. She was not having any luck. She was sitting in her van at the mall, eating a chicken sandwich, when she spied Duncan coming out with his arms loaded.

She reached out and found out that he was there to pick up the tuxes for him, Colin, and Mr. MacManus. They had been altered by a specialty shop inside one of the shops that she had just been in. She jumped from her vehicle and followed him. Certainly, a person who knew about tuxes knew where one could buy a stupid dress for this thing, wouldn't they?

"Mr. Duncan?" He turned quickly at her greeting, startling her.

"Goodness, Miss Sara, I did not see you coming. How are you, dear? Fine, I hope." His smile was just what she needed to bolster her feelings.

"Fine, I'm fine. I was wondering if you had a minute or two you could spare me, please? It's about this dinner thingy with Blood...Mr. MacManus. First, I was wondering about the dinner part. I'm not...you know, part of the dinner, am I? I mean, they're calling it a dinner and all. So...?" She shuddered a little. Maybe if she was part of his dinner, it wouldn't be so very bad. Damn it. More and more thoughts like that kept popping up, and she was gonna seek professional help, she thought.

"Oh no, miss. It is nothing like that at all. It is called a dinner because a great many of our kind have humans working for them who are not aware of what they are. It is just a courtesy for them. Understand?" She nodded, relieved. "Good, what else may I endeavor to assist you with?"

Okay, endeavor? He needed to get out more and meet more people, she thought, but then she decided that she liked him very much the way he was, eccentric or not.

"Mr. MacManus wants me to be his guard Friday night. I...I mean, do you know where I can find a suitable dress? I don't know a flippin' thing about fashion, even less about shoes and stuff. I really don't have a great deal of money to spend, just about eight hundred dollars, I guess."

Sara really didn't know fashion and wasn't sure if what she had to spend was a little or a lot. Mrs. Carlovetti had spent over two thousand on her dress alone and another three hundred on shoes.

"I do know a couple of reputable places we can look. There are also a couple more that are second-hand shops. Which would you prefer?" he asked as he opened his car door.

"If you don't mind, just give me the address to both places, please? I can go and look to see what I can get for my money. I'm sure they'll have something I can use."

Second-hand sounded okay to her. The dresses would be much cheaper now that someone had already worn them. She hoped so anyway…even with the added cost of dry-cleaning, the price difference would make it well worth going to the second-hand shops first.

"One of the places is owned and operated by one of our kind, so maybe we could manage a discount from them. We will see what we can work out, shall we? Two places deal in antique dresses that I think might suit you. We should go to those first, I think."

"Oh, no, Mr. Duncan. No, you don't have to go. I can manage by myself. I'm sure you have plenty to do for this shindig. I wouldn't want to take you from your job."

Oh no, she thought, *he can't mean to go.* She was nervous enough as it was being a guard again. Plus, she needed to do this on her own as she did all things.

"Nonsense, come along. Now, I just need to put these suits in my car. You can either ride with me or follow. Which would you prefer?"

Sara saw by the look on his face that he was not going to be deterred. She knew how to buy clothes. Just go in, get what you want, pay, then leave. Walmart always had what she needed, but somehow, she didn't think this would be quite so easy.

Sara had watched women in the couple of shops she had been in. It was mind boggling how much crap went with a simple dress. She looked at him again. Surely, after all this time, he would be better at this business than she would be.

"If you don't mind, I'll follow you. That way, if you need to go or get called away, you won't have to worry about me. Mr. Duncan, are you sure you won't get into hot water with the big guy? He can be sorta...well, he is very bossy, as I'm sure you know." She could only hope that he was called away, and then he would not need to explain why he was helping her out again to his master.

"No, miss. He'll be happy that I was able to assist you once again. And I believe I will enjoy this excursion as well. Shall we?"

They loaded the garment bags into this monster Hummer and went to get her van. He drove her over to it, and then off they went to Vintage Wears in downtown Zanesville, a beautiful shop that dealt in antique dresses and apparel.

~~~

"Sire, it's Duncan."

Aaron smiled. He had expected this call since he had found the note Duncan had left him in the kitchen telling him that he'd gone to the mall to get the "tuxedos and finery." Duncan rarely drove, and he had taken the Hummer to the mall. A deadly combination if there ever was one.

"Yes, Duncan, having trouble with the Hummer again? I told you to practice more before going to the mall; it's a nightmarish place for even a good driver."

"No, sir, I've met up with Miss Sara, and she has asked for my help. It seems that she is in need of my help knowing where to find a dress suitable enough to be your guard at the dinner Friday. She also seemed to be under the misconception that she was to be a part of the menu, if not the whole menu. I have explained that part to her to both your satisfaction, I believe.

We are out shopping for a dress as we speak. She thought that I should inform you, as I will be later than the time I allotted myself to be back to the mansion."

"My guard, huh? Where is she?"

He wasn't going to think about her and menus; about sinking his teeth into her creamy neck as his aperitif. Nor about how taking her as his main course, all of her body spread before him on his bed. Damn, he really was in bad shape here, he thought, as he adjusted himself for perhaps the hundredth time today.

"She is following me in her van," Duncan said. "She is just behind me."

"I never thought about her clothing when I asked her." Aaron had a horrible thought. "Christ, she is not going to buy a t-shirt and cut-offs, is she? Duncan, please, make sure that she wears a dress. I will, of course, pay for anything she needs. You have my credit cards; make sure that I get the bill, Duncan."

"Sir, I do not think that would be a good idea. I believe Miss Sara has a great deal of pride and would…how should I say this… ah, yes, bristle at the idea of you buying her clothing. We are on our way to a little shop I know in order to purchase me a little time to speak to you."

"Bristle?" Aaron snorted at that. "That would be an understatement, I believe. What's really going on, Duncan? Because I'm sure, you didn't call me to make me feel guilty about this. I know that she doesn't have any money for this, so just what do you have in mind?" Bristle. He would be lucky if she didn't stake him while he slept.

"I do not believe my paying for her purchases will be wise for either of us, sire. She would most definitely have a fit of major proportions, I think." *Duncan couldn't be more right,* Aaron thought. "No, it would be very beneficial for all concerned if you were to make a phone call to a place called Other Worldly Creations and see if the proprietor would be willing to cut the new master a favor, so to speak. I'm sure you can handle the details of the transaction, can you not?"

There was a tone there, but Aaron wasn't about to point it out to the man. He was doing him a favor by letting him know about her financial situation. He was still trying to track down who she was providing for in Nevada.

"Yes, I think I can handle it. You are a wily one, Duncan. However did I miss that?" he asked sarcastically, though it usually went over Duncan's head.

"I believe I'm getting better with age, sir. You can only expect more in the ensuing years. Do be quick about the call, sir. We are nearly at our first adventure. We should be at the shop in less than an hour."

Aaron disconnected the call and went to find the phone numbers he had seen just recently. He had found the file cabinet with all the names of the proprietors of every vampire-owned business in his realm just yesterday. He had been hiding from Sara and thought to clean up the desk when he came across it.

"Yes. Hello, this is Aaron MacManus. I'd like to speak with...." He looked down at the file in front of him. "Elaina Spencer, please."

"If this is you, Daphne, I don't think this is the least bit funny. I don't need the added stress of you pretending to be the new bastard in my life I like to refer to as hell."

Aaron did not say anything. He was not even sure what to say. He was just about to hang up and call Duncan back when the voice spoke again.

"Please tell me this is Daphne, and it's a joke. I'll laugh. I'll think it's as funny as you want me to," the woman begged.

"No, I'm not Daphne, and it frightens me on many levels that you think that I sound like her or her me. Laughing won't be necessary either. I'm not usually thought of as funny anyway. I'd like to speak to Ms. Spencer. Is she around?"

Duncan said they would be there soon, and Aaron wanted to get this taken care of before they arrived. He had to arrange his end of the shopping trip or have Duncan upset with him.

"Master, I'm very sorry. I had no...I beg you not to hurt my employees. They had nothing to do with my behavior. Some of them are humans. Please, master."

Aaron leaned back in his chair and contemplated finding the previous master's ashes and killing him again. This would be funny if it was not so frustrating.

"Ms. Spencer, I presume. I don't make a habit of harming people, human or otherwise, because you thought a joke was being played on you. I have a friend coming to your shop, and I...."

"She'll have whatever she wants. No charge. My shop also has a line of naughty clothes. I just got in a French maid's outfit. Just tell me what you want her to look like, and I'll make sure it happens." She was gushing, and Aaron could barely think.

The thought of Sara in a short maid's dress distracted him momentarily, and Aaron reached down to adjust his cock. He was going to be permanently bruised. He just knew it. He shifted in his seat and finally had to stand up. His erection was so painful. He thought that it was a small miracle that he could even think at all, what with his blood always pooled in his groin.

"No, no outfits, please." He took a deep breath before he could continue. "She needs a dress, a formal dress. It's for the pledge dinner. And I will be paying the bills. But I don't want her to know. Can you arrange that for me?" Maybe he should have her wrapped in a toga. The more of her covered, the better.

"You'll pay for it? I don't understand. Oh! I see you want me to pretend you have an account with us. I can do that. Usually, I just give them what they want, but if you want her to think you're paying, I can—"

"No, you don't...I actually want to pay for whatever she picks. Just, I don't want her to know. Duncan, the man that'll be with her, he'll have a credit card. Just let him pay for it, and it'll be fine."

"What happens if she doesn't find anything? Then what?" Elaina suddenly sounded resigned. "I mean, will you give me time to relocate my people before this Duncan does his part and kills me?" Christ, even dead Carlos was certainly making his life difficult.

"Ms. Spencer—Elaina—my date, and Duncan will be there in a few minutes. I want you to sell her whatever she needs to wear to a formal function; dress, stockings, shoes, everything. Then I want you to charge my credit card for it. The full price. If she doesn't find anything she likes, then she'll move to another shop." He could only hope she found something there; he did not want to do this again. "I swear to you that it'll be no reflection on you. No harm will come to you or your employees. Sara is a very nice woman. She only gets mad at me when she gets her panties in a twist. Well, there was that time with Colin, but he started...I digress. I assure you, as your master, you are safe."

Aaron didn't think he convinced her of anything as he hung up the phone other than someone was coming by her shop, who may or may not buy a dress, which may or may not get her killed and that she was to charge it to an account that may or may not be real. If there was ever a time in his life as a vampire, this was the one time he really could use a stiff drink. He looked at the clock and realized Duncan and Sara were probably already there. *Christ*, he thought again, *I hope Sara doesn't kill me for this.* He smiled. Maybe he would just go there soon and purchase her the little maid's outfit and see what else they might have in the naughty section.

CHAPTER ELEVEN

Sara felt the terror and hatred slap her hard as soon as she walked into the lovely shop. She gently reached out to find the source and was surprised by what she found. So Aaron was paying for her clothes, and Duncan, now that she looked into him, had arranged the whole thing. Damn it. The entire store was in a mental meltdown, waiting for the axe to befall the vampire and the human employees working there. She gave a small push to the woman, relaxing her somewhat.

"Hello, I'm Sara Temple. I'm going to be an escort for your master at the dinner Friday night." Sara held out her hand as she moved toward the woman, who seemed to be radiating with anger. "I need a dress for the event and was wondering if you could please help me. I'll be honest; I don't go out much — actually, never. I know absolutely nothing about dressing up, not enough to not embarrass anyone, anyway. I don't know what it'll take to make me look presentable. I'm not even sure of my size or anything."

Elaina moved forward to take Sara's hand. There was confusion as well as surprise written all over the vampire's face. *Good*, Sara thought, *one good thing at a time.*

"I'm Elaina Spencer. I'm the owner. Let's see what we can do for you. I think we should get you to a dressing room and size you up. That will give us a better idea of what we have to work with, okay?"

Elaina's voice was sharp and a little condescending. Sara was not offended. If the arrogant men would have stayed out of this, the poor woman would have been fine.

Sara was ushered off to a beautifully appointed pink dressing room, where she was asked to strip down to her underclothes to be measured. The room only had one small mirror, but it had the most gorgeous fainting couch she'd ever seen. It was of the deepest red, almost a blood red, with two floral pillows that had been beaded and stitched by hand.

Sara's wounds had healed nicely, and since she had not met up with her tormentor in a few weeks, her bruises were actually all gone. She was glad; she did not want nor need any embarrassing questions right now. And right now, she had to deal with Duncan while she waited for Elaina to bring her some things to try on.

"*Mr. Duncan,*" she whispered through his mind. "*I'm not at all happy with you right now.*"

"Miss?" he said out loud. In her anger, she had forgotten he might be surprised by her talking to him in his mind.

"*I'm in the dressing room, so speak to me mentally, please. I don't know when you called your master and arranged this shopping spree, but you shouldn't have. Do you know what this has done to this poor woman? She believes I'm here to get a dress or have her and her employees killed if they don't make me happy.*" She laid her hand over her bared belly when she thought about the rest of their assumption. "*They also believe that your master is my lover, and he is fulfilling one of my wildest dreams...of owning a dress made by a vampire. How sick is that, I ask you? No, don't answer that. I'm upset with you both right now.*"

"I'm sorry, miss." He sounded contrite. Well, she was pissed, damn it. "*Truly, I am. I only meant to help you. I know that you are low on funds. And the master did ask you to go, did he not? He is very happy to purchase what you need. In fact, he felt quite bad for not thinking to tell you so when he asked you to begin with.*"

"*Does he normally pay for the dresses of women he invites out?*" Hurt, and something else she didn't want to analyze when she thought of him buying things for other women, she tried her best to sound like having men buy her dresses wasn't that big of a deal. *"Please don't answer that. I don't want to know what he pays for or who he pays for. I'll play the part of the helpless woman this time, and I'll go so far as to assure Elaina that her new master is a kind and gentle man, no matter how much it makes me want to puke. But, Duncan, understand this, you've hurt me. I came to you for help, not a handout. I won't make the same mistake again."*

Sara angrily brushed at the tears as she closed the connection between them. She would not hold a grudge. It was not in her nature. But to think that Aaron knew of her situation hurt her somehow.

Sara walked out of the dressing room some forty minutes later with the gown Elaina had said would suit. She walked to the three-way mirrors and looked at the person staring back at her. Elaina was just behind her, fluffing out the back just a little. The dress was magnificent, and it fit Sara as if it had been made with her in mind, both in style, color, and size.

"Oh my." Sara could not believe that that was her staring back from the mirrors. Elaina walked up to her and twisted her hair up and off her neck. It bared her shoulders and long neck, making the dress look all the more exotic.

"Yes, and what an understatement that is. Miss Temple, if you don't mind my saying so, you look beautiful."

Sara grinned at her and turned right and left to see the whole of her reflection. The dress made her feel beautiful too, something she couldn't remember ever feeling before. She wondered what Aaron would think of it, wondered if he would think she was beautiful. She suddenly realized where her thoughts were and abruptly shut that train of thought down.

The dress was an array of dark greens, starting with the strapless green velvet that made up the top of the gown. It showed off an ample amount of her breasts that were pushed up and together to show the spectacular cleavage that Sara already had. The form-fitting bodice and waist hugged her smallish figure with braids of dyed green leather crisscrossed across her flat tummy and then attached to the gauzy material that hung from her hips and flared out to the floor. The dress emphasized her willowy body, as well as showing off her unadorned neck. The elbow-length black gloves were the finishing touch to the elegance and beauty.

"You'll need to wear your hair up and swept away from your face like this. I wouldn't wear anything else, no jewelry at all." Elaina winked at Sara in the mirror as she continued. "I've seen other women try that dress on, and I thought they looked okay in it. But you, Miss Sara, you are that dress."

"Thank you, thank you so much. I didn't know I could look so pretty. The dress does wonders, doesn't it?"

Elaina showed her how to do a simple twist in her hair. It was just a fancy way to pull her braid up and off her neck. She was a little embarrassed by the amount of her breasts that seemed to almost spill over the top of the bodice and tugged at it again. Elaina smacked her hand away gently with a grin.

"Leave it alone. You look lovely, and there isn't so much of you showing that you need to keep trying to put it away."

Sara saw Duncan looking at her in the reflection of the mirror. Apparently, so did Elaina.

"So, what do you think, Mr. Duncan? Will she be the hit of the ball?"

"It is not a ball, Ms. Spencer. It is just the dinner. And she will be the most beautiful woman there, I believe."

Sara flushed deeply at his words. She retreated to the dressing room to change back into her street clothes. First, however, she sat down on the couch. She was suddenly afraid…afraid of what Aaron would think about her in the dress. What if he thought she looked to be playing dress up and should have tried something else? What if he thought that she was ridiculous looking or that she was not pretty enough now to be his…date?

"There won't be a charge. I want her to have the dress. No one will be able to look nearly that lovely in it, and I won't have another woman even trying to." She overheard Elaina tell Duncan this just as she stepped out of the little room.

"Oh no, miss. That is not what the master wanted. He wants to pay for the dress. It was never his intention of taking the dress, I assure you." Sara frowned at the wording of what he said but was not going to worry overly much about that right now. It was Duncan, she thought.

"Yes, I'm aware of that now. But there still won't be a charge for her dress," Elaina said again.

"Then I won't take it," Sara told her as she approached the counter. "I'm sure that I can find another dress, not near as lovely, but I won't take this from you without paying for it. Even I can see that this is hand stitched. You also have a good many hours in just the beading alone, no doubt. No, I'm sorry, I can't let you do that. I won't let you do it. You are in business to make money, and if I ever require another dress, I want to be able to come back here to get one. I will also want to be able to send anyone who asks about this dress to you, and I won't be able to do that if you are out of business, now will I? No, you charge Mr. MacManus for the cost of the dress, the real price, or I go elsewhere." She regretfully laid the dress across the counter and turned to leave.

So Elaina sold the dress to Mr. A. MacManus for what would be three months' salary for Sara. She was staggered at the amount but steeled herself with the knowledge that somehow, she would pay the stupid man back.

As they turned to leave the store, Elaina stopped her again, only this time with a gentle tug on her arm. "Thank you very much, Miss Sara. You have restored my faith in my kind. Would you be so kind as to tell the master that it was my honor and pleasure to serve him through you, and I will be the first in line to pledge to him tomorrow night?"

"Yes, I will. Please, I'd like for you to call me Sara. Thank you, and I will see you tomorrow night."

Sara hurried to her van, carrying her garment bag and the smaller bag containing the shoes, stockings, gloves, and hair clips. She was reaching into the large slider door when she looked over at Duncan.

"Miss, I would beg your forgiveness. I was wrong."

She wanted to tell him it was okay, not to worry about it, but it was not. She was getting tired of these guys running her life. "Yes, you were. But I wouldn't have gotten to meet Elaina or have gotten this dress if you hadn't been so high-handed. So, I forgive you. But Mr. Duncan, know this, I won't be so forgiving next time. You had no right to tell him of my financial needs. Again, I wouldn't have been able to get this dress without his help, but I assure you, I would not have embarrassed him in any way by my dress or my actions if that's what concerned him."

"No, miss, I assure you that was not my intention when I telephoned him. No, I only meant to lessen your burden in your time of need. I am sorry if that is what you thought," he said in earnest.

"It doesn't matter now. But please let him know that I will pay him back every penny he spent. I do not want to feel obligated to him or anyone else. I pay my way. Understand?"

"The master will not be happy about that," Duncan said with a sly smile. "He will be mad enough to know that you found out what we were up to tonight. More so that you know how much the dress actually cost him."

She looked at Duncan and realized he was going to enjoy telling his master what she had said. She grinned broadly at him. "I'm sure his ego will be able to take it. It's certainly big enough. Now, if you don't mind, I need to go and park. I'm tired, and I have to go to work in a few hours. You should hurry home. I'm sure he is chomping at the bit, wearing down his fangs, wondering what you are doing out so late." She started to shake his hand and put hers out to do so when he suddenly turned it over and kissed the back of it. "Duncan, thank you very much for your help. I couldn't have done this without you."

~~~

"Would you like to see my dress? It's quite nice. Well, it should be for the amount it cost." Sara contacted Mel as soon as she got back to the wooded preserve.

"Yes, show me."

Sara thought about what she had looked like in the mirrors and sent the image to her friend.

"Oh my goddess, Sara, you're even more beautiful than I remember. When did you grow up?"

"You are so very funny today, aren't you? But isn't it nice? I hope I don't fall off the shoes that go with it. That's all I need."

"You'll do just fine, have faith. Besides, no one is going to care if you hobble all night long once they see that lovely neck of yours."

Aaron, she thought, what will he think of my neck? She tingled all over at the thought. *"What is it, what's happened?"* Sara could feel the tension in Mel's voice and, with a quick scan, could tell that it was not just in her voice; her whole body was nearly brittle with it.

"I'm stronger now, Sara. It's time for me to show myself again. The world needs this magic, and we need to show them that they are not alone in this world. It's been too long already."

Sara did not say anything for some seconds; she'd known this day was coming. She had been wondering when Mel was going to make the decision. She just hoped it would have been later rather than sooner. Sara had failed her once, and she was not ready to be put to the test again. Not yet, anyway.

"You know I will continue to protect you no matter what you decide, now or later. You are my queen first and my friend always. Please, Mel, don't do this because you think to lessen my involvement. I'll always be there for you."

"I know that, Sara. I'll need to show myself soon, very soon, I'm afraid. Changes need to be made, Sara. I'm not the same queen I was

when you put me here to rest. I've made some decisions that will affect a great many people, you especially. You have sacrificed so much for me and our magic. My first priority is to have you exonerated of all charges as well as those who fell to save me. You need to be recognized for what you did. Then I'll need to deal with Sherman. It's time for that as well."

Sara was afraid for Mel. And then she wondered if Mel realized that she was not the same either. *"I never expected anything from you."* She had been working too. *"Nor do I now. I didn't do anything that anyone else wouldn't have done. I've given up nothing that you wouldn't have done for me. As for Sherman, you aren't to worry about him until you're stronger. I've been working on my powers daily, and he won't get the better of me again."* Amazingly enough, since meeting Aaron, she had wanted to be better at a lot of things.

"Oh Sara, do you think I wanted you to give up your life to hide away from everyone so you could shelter me? Do you think I like knowing that you have been paying so much money to have me protected and taken care of while I healed? No, love. Never." Sara could feel Mel's anger even over the long distance. *"My duty as your queen was to be the one offering and guaranteeing your safety, not the other way around. I know you aren't going to like what I've done, but I have decreed it to be so. When we finally get to talk, you will begin to understand what I have decided."*

Sara was reasonably sure she was not going to like whatever it was. It angered her that Mel was making decisions on her behalf without asking. It reminded her of someone else in her life, she thought with a grimace.

"I have to go to sleep now," Sara told her. *"I'm mad, as I'm sure you are aware. I've had a really long day and need to rest."*

"Goodnight, Sara. I love you, daughter of my heart." Sara felt the warmth Mel sent her, but she was too pissed off to acknowledge it.

"I love you too, my queen."

CHAPTER TWELVE

Aaron watched as she walked into the office the next morning and stopped dead when she saw him sitting in her chair. Not exactly the reception he was hoping for.

"You might as well come on over. We have a lot to go over before tonight, and I still have to travel back home," he told her.

"You said that you were going to call. I'm reasonably sure whatever you have to say to me could have been said over the phone. In fact, I would prefer it that way." She didn't move from her position when she asked, "Why are you here?"

"I just wanted to see your lovely face again, isn't that enough?" Her glare nearly made him laugh. "No, I can see you don't believe me. Oh well, have a seat. Let's get tonight finalized. I will have a car pick you up at your home at four o'clock. I've already asked and found out the Carlovettis are closing at two, so that will give you plenty of time to get there and wait for the driver. What is your address, by the way? All I've been able to find is a post office box number."

Aaron picked up a pen off the desk she had been using. It smelled of her, he had discovered. It was a very neat desk, everything in its place. He wondered if she would be willing to help with his at home. *Nah*, he thought, *she would probably set fire to it and start over*, which, come to think of it, was not a bad idea.

"No, I'll drive myself. I'm quite capable of getting to and from there on my own. You know, I have had a life up until you," she told him. Quite impertinently, too, he thought.

"Have you noticed that you are forever saying 'no' to me? It's getting quite old." He leaned back in the chair. "Now, as I was saying...no, you won't drive yourself there. Someone will pick you up. Where do you live? I'm quite serious about this, Sara. Tell me."

"Did you ever think to listen when I say 'no' to you? I doubt you think you're ever wrong either, do you?" She flopped down in the other chair before she told him, "I live two point three miles from here, due west. I can give you the longitude and latitude if you'd like. Let me see, for Columbus, where you live, it's thirty-nine degrees north by eighty-three degrees, zero minutes west. Now where I live, it's a little different. It's forty degrees, four minutes, fourteen seconds north by eighty-two degrees, ten minutes, thirty-three seconds west. Is that specific enough for you, your dickship?"

"That's very funny. Don't be a smart ass, Sara. What is your physical address?" She looked away from him and out the window just over his shoulder. This is not going to be good. Deep in his bones, he knew without a doubt that whatever she was trying to avoid telling him, he was not going to like. "Sara?"

"There isn't an actual address there. I just know where it is. I...like it there, it's very quiet." She turned and glared at him as if to say he was the cause of all the noise in her life.

"How quiet, and what does the house look like?" His head was beginning to ache again. He had lived for over fourteen hundred years, and in only two weeks of knowing her, he wanted an aspirin and hard liquor, not necessarily in that order.

"There isn't a house," she said quietly, still not looking at him.

"The apartment then, or trailer. What's the building look like that you are staying in?" He was so frustrated, which, to his way of thinking, was a foregone conclusion when talking with her.

"There isn't a building there, none of any kind. There might have been at one time, I suppose. I think I saw a foundation once when I was on my way to the little creek."

He stared at her for a full minute. "Are you telling me you are sleeping outside? Are you kidding me?"

"No."

"No, what?" He didn't even try to hide his anger. "You aren't sleeping outside, or no, you're not kidding me? Which is it? Because either one you answer 'no' to is gonna piss me off."

"Like there's a big surprise," she snarled at him. "You get pissed about everything. And the answer is 'no' to both. No, I'm not sleeping outside, and no, I'm not kidding you. At least I'm not sleeping outside right now."

"Where exactly are you sleeping?" he asked her quietly.

"In my van."

"How long?" His head was now at the about to explode stage. His eye started to twitch a little too.

"I don't know, about eight feet long, I guess." She grinned at him then. "Shall I satisfy your curiosity and go out and measure it for you?" She had a tone. She had the nerve to have a tone with him!

He slammed both hands down on the desk as he rose over her, making her jump.

"How long...have you...been sleeping...in your van?" He said each word slowly, and each one enunciated so as she would not misunderstand what he was asking her. He was beyond mad at this point and wanted her to answer the damned question.

"Since it got warm again, March twenty-second." She stood too, her anger evident in every part of her lovely body. "I don't really keep track of the precise date. Do you know the date of things you do? Yes, you probably have this note pad just filled with stupid information like that."

"Again? Where were you sleeping during the previous months, and I can only assume that it was during the winter months, correct?" He moved away from her before he did something stupid...like pull her over the table and claim her, drink from her, strip her down, and fuck her.

He wasn't going to justify his notebooks of dates to her. He began to pace. She just would not understand. Sometimes, to be honest neither did he, but that was beside the point.

"Yes, the YWCA. They have rooms to let for a low price." As if that should explain everything to him. He stopped pacing.

"And again, meaning that you have been doing this for a number of years, also correct?"

"Yes," she hissed at him. "Not that it's any of your business, but four."

"Four. Four years. You've been living out of your van for four years, and you didn't think to tell anyone?" He needed a drink… not just a drink, he thought, but the entire bottle. No, maybe the entire keg, maybe that would be enough.

"Tell anyone what?" she asked him. "It isn't anyone's business where I live, what I do, not so long as I do my job. And I do my job. I'm very good at it too."

He turned and stared at her. She was serious, he realized. She actually believed that it wouldn't be a problem to anyone, her living in the wilderness alone.

"You don't think anyone would care enough about you to want to know this information?" he said softly. "That, like you said, as long as you were doing your job, it would be okay with them? Okay, that you were out there unprotected, alone, just three miles down the road? That you'd have no heat, no way to cook? Where did you bathe…the creek?" He paused when she flushed. "You bathed in a creek bed?" he shouted.

"Two point three miles, not three," she corrected. "If you're gonna yell at me, get your facts straight."

He roared. Three pilots came rushing into the room to see what animal he was torturing. Mrs. Davis, one of the cleaning crew ladies, crossed herself and said two Hail Marys as she came to a screaming halt just inside the doorway.

"Get out!" he roared at the room. Then, just as quickly as

they entered, they ran out again.

His eyes had turned in his anger; his fangs had dropped as well. He knew this because he could see the red haze through his eyes, her body, and her anger, brighter to him. He felt his fangs explode from his gums. He wanted to bite, to take, to make her body his. His heart was pounding, and his blood was roaring hotly through his veins. He did not think he had ever been so pissed in his entire life.

"Sara." When she started to say something, he raised his hand. "No, don't speak. I don't know what I'll do to you if you say one thing more." He took a deep breath, then another. "There will be a car out front at two o'clock to pick you up. They will deliver you and all your belongings to my house. If for any reason whatsoever you are not here to go, I will punish the driver. Do I make myself clear?" Even in his anger, he knew that threatening her personally would do no good.

"I'm not a child, and I'd appreciate it if you'd just mind your own fucking business. I don't need you to treat—"

He cut her off before he did something drastic. "You should really shut up now. I'm not finished." He took a deep breath before he continued. "Another driver will bring your home to the estate, and you will remain a guest in my home until such time I see fit to let you go, if ever. You are a danger to yourself, and if I have to have you declared unstable, I will. You need a keeper, and you are going to get one."

"You bastard. I really hate you," she snarled at him.

"Yes, and with all probability, you will even more so before this is over. You will not run, Sara, or so help me when I catch you—and I will, make no mistake about that—I will make you very sorry. You hear me?"

"Yes," she hissed at him. "You're a prick. I hope you know that."

"Nice. Very mature. Polite, and name-calling too. Now, be a good girl and do as you're told. I will see you this evening." With that, he turned and left.

Sara sat down in the desk chair and burst into tears for the second time since meeting with the overbearing vampire.

~~~

At five minutes until two, two werewolves showed up at the hangar to do just what Aaron told her they would. When the younger man asked for her van keys to drive it to the estate, she refused to give them to him. He did not even bat an eye, turned, broke into the driver's side door, hotwired the ignition, and drove off as simple as you please.

The older man looked at her. "You can either get into that monstrosity of a vehicle all by your sweet little self or...and I gotta tell you, I'm hoping you opt for door number two here...I throw your cute little butt up over my shoulder and carry you to it. It don't matter none to me, darlin'." He grinned at her, showing her just a little of his canines.

Mustering as much dignity as she could, she snatched up her backpack and followed him out to a dark green Hummer. When he opened the back door for her to enter the dark car, she looked at him, pulled open the front passenger door, and got in. She heard him laugh, and that made her angrier.

"The man said you'd be madder than a hornet, but you'd be polite to me. I gotta hand it to you, little lady, you sure have him all in a twist." She looked at the man, wondering if he was angry at her for making the vamp mad. He looked genuinely amused by it.

"Good," she said. She did not say another word all the way to Columbus.

The wolf threw back his head and laughed. And he continued to laugh all the way to the estate.

CHAPTER THIRTEEN

Aaron was in his lair, well beneath the main house, when quite suddenly, he was awake. No one, not even Duncan, could get into those rooms without his permission, but something, or someone, had woken him from his deep, healing sleep.

"Who's there? Where are you?" He sat up cautiously, pulling the silk sheet over his bare body.

"I am Melody, Mistress of Light, and Keeper of All Magic. I have a need of you, Aaron Xavier MacManus, and would like to speak to you privately, please."

The room suddenly became ablaze with candlelight. As soon as his eyes adjusted to the soft glow, Aaron spied a tiny woman sitting,…well, on closer inspection, floating…above the armchair across the room from his bed.

"How did you get in here?" *Or better yet,* he thought, *why are you here in my lair?*

"Actually, I'm not really here. I'm in Nevada, Reno, actually. Have you ever been there? It's very hot, but the room I have is quite lovely. I'll only be there for a short time more before I move back to Molavonta." She smiled at him. "I'm hiding, you see. I wanted to see you to see your worth before I came to talk to you personally. I hope you don't mind."

She got up and floated toward the dresser closest to where she sat. He watched as she leaned down and looked at the photos on it.

Most of the pictures had been taken by Duncan. They were of

him and his friends over the centuries. His favorite one, the one of him and Duncan together in the early nineteen hundreds, she now held in her hand.

"You aren't here, yet you can see me and I you," Aaron said, more to himself than to her. "You can pick up things too. How is that even possible?"

After setting the gold frame back down on the dresser, she moved over to the suit of armor that graced the far corner of the room. He had worn that particular suit during the Crusades in the thirteenth century when he fought for the Holy Land versus Muslims. He had been a Templar Knight. He had just avoided being arrested with Jacques de Molay, the Grand Master of the Knights Templar, and sixty of his senior knights in Paris that night on October thirteenth.

The men and Jacques had been charged with heresy and accused of homosexual acts, crimes punishable by death. The admissions of guilt were extracted with the use of torture. The pope initiated inquiries into the order, and thousands of Knights Templar were arrested across Europe. Aaron had been away in America and not a part of the group that fateful night. When word had reached him of what happened, it was too late for him to help. He kept the armor as part of respect for the last Master of the Knights.

"I'm magic," she told him without turning. "It's as simple as that. You are Sara's vampire, are you not? She didn't tell me how big you were, but then she isn't very little herself, is she? I've come to talk to you about her."

"Sara told you about me?" Aaron didn't like the sound of that. "Not everything she said can be held against me. She and I haven't seen eye to eye on much since our acquaintance. Really, I don't think we've agreed on one thing since we've met. Did you know that she is living in her car? Stupid girl, what does she want? To get killed? Well, that could be her intention, as she has asked me to end her life before. But she did say that it was a lapse in judgment, so perhaps she's changed her mind about that." He stopped talking when he realized the woman was staring at him quite alarmingly. Oh, maybe she did not know about his and Sara's little conversation when they met.

"I do now, thank you. Did she tell you who beat her up? No, I can see that she didn't. I won't either. Tell you, I mean, at least not until I get to know you a little better. As a matter of fact, I only just found out myself, by accident." She sat over the chair again. "Now, I want to tell you a few things, ask you some others, and see what we can come up with, vamp."

He leaned back on the headboard to his bed. He figured they were going to be a while if they were going to try and understand Sara. The woman across from him laughed.

"You might be right on that. But she is a good person." Mel grinned. "And quite stubborn, too. She will make you a good mate if you want her."

"You read minds too." He marveled how he had not felt the slightest intrusion from her touch. Then he realized something else. "You're the one she's protecting out west."

"Very good, vamp. Yes. Sara's been hiding me away for some time now. She's been waiting for me to heal, to get stronger," she told him. "Sara has sacrificed so much to keep me safe. Now I'd like to make sure she is safe as well."

He stiffened at that. Sara was his to protect. Sara was his. "Tell me who is beating her. I'm assuming it's the same one she's protecting you from, right?" Mel nodded at his question. "She's mine to...Sara's my mate, as you've said. I need to protect her." He felt her this time. Her touch moved through his mind through his memories. He let her.

"Well, Aaron Xavier MacManus, let's you and I talk about the stubbornly beautiful Sara Temple, shall we?" Then she looked away from him for a moment. "You will know that the man she is protecting me from isn't her only tormentor. I will not give you the other because it is not safe for too many others just yet."

It was nearly sunset when she faded away. Aaron fell into a deep sleep once again, wondering as he drifted off if it had all been a dream.

<div align="center">~~~</div>

"Is she here?" Aaron asked Duncan as soon as he walked into the kitchen. Aaron felt...rejuvenated and alive like he had gotten a shiny new toy for Christmas. Too bad this toy was extremely powerful and pissed off at him as well. Well, he thought, she had really left him with nothing more to do than he'd done.

"You gave her little to no choice in the matter, my lord," Duncan told him with a sad look. "You had a werewolf pick her up and bring her here as if she was something you picked from a catalog. Of course, she is here."

"I couldn't let her live in her car, Duncan. It isn't safe, not even for her. Surely you can see that? I had to do something. Did William have any trouble with her?"

Aaron had met William Daniels a few months ago while out walking in the moonlight. He had been stalking a deer on the property just beyond his. William had shifted to human from wolf as soon as he had seen Aaron coming toward him. It was a courtesy to let one supernatural know that you were not hiding to cause the other harm. Aaron had been using him as muscle ever since.

"No, sir. No trouble whatsoever. He said that he had never enjoyed doing an errand so much and that he thought about paying you to let him fetch you a human more often. I did explain to him the circumstances surrounding the 'fetching' of the young miss. It upset him a bit that she had been out when he could have been keeping an eye on her. He said that she is too...let me see...'too prime to be out alone.' He was quite taken with the little miss, it seems."

"Hmmm, so long as he's taken with her from a distance, I don't care. Duncan, there is something I've been meaning to tell you for a few days now. It's about Sara. I know you like her. I'm glad for that. I don't know for sure, but, well…."

"She's your mate, sire?"

Aaron looked up sharply at the man. Duncan really had become quite wily indeed. "I…how did…yes." Aaron threw his hands into the air. "I believe Sara is my mate. Why is that the first guess everyone makes concerning her and I?"

"How do you feel about that, sir, if you do not mind my asking?" It was a good question, one he had been asking himself for two days.

"I don't know. Ask me after tonight. That is if I'm still alive. She may be the death of me yet." He patted his good friend on the back and went in search of Sara.

CHAPTER FOURTEEN

Sara was just getting into the huge garden tub in the bathroom when she heard footsteps coming down the hallway. There was only one person she could think of who walked like that, and she really did not want to see him. Not now — likely, not ever.

As she lay in the warm water, she thought about Aaron. Did she really hate him? Yes...no...maybe. Okay, maybe she didn't hate him, but she didn't like him either. At least she didn't want to like him. He was overbearing and arrogant. But he did have her safety in mind. And he was incredibly handsome and sweet — sometimes. There were times when he was yelling at her, she never knew whether she really wanted to smack him or pull him into her arms and...what? Strangle him? Possibly. It sounded like a good idea. She could see herself wrapping her arms around his neck, her fingers touching the back of his hair, squeezing him until he came close to her. Her mouth, maybe.

Frustrated, she got out of the tub and began drying herself vigorously. Damned man had her so upset she didn't know which way was up or down. And now...and now he was coming into the room.

The bedroom to which she had been taken when she arrived this afternoon was different than the one that she had been in previously. This one was elegant and bright. Not that the other room wasn't nice, but this room, she loved.

The bed was an oversized king canopy with an ecru-colored lacey cover over the top. The four posts that held it in place were dark cherry and fashioned with pineapples carved into them just at eye level. The coverlet was done in an array of pinks and purple velvets and then accented with embroidered flowers at each corner of the six by six squares. The furniture was also cherry, a large dresser she thought was called a highboy, and a vanity with a smallish chair with a cushion covered in the same pattern as the spread. No curtains were adorning the three floor-to-ceiling windows. In their place were shutters of the same dark cherry as the furniture. The hardwood floor had a beautiful wool rug with the same motif as the rest of the room. Sara was just tying the white chenille robe when Aaron stepped through the open door.

"Are you still angry with me?" She ignored his question. "You have to realize, Sara, how lucky you were that you'd not been raped or murdered out there alone."

She just glared at him, walked to the vanity, and sat down. "I'm getting dressed. Go away."

She had made the decision while trying to relax in the tub to no longer be polite to him. It was dangerous, she thought. Not that she had been over effervescent to begin with, but now she was not holding back, damn it. She thought it might be necessary to keep her sanity.

"I've come to talk to you," he said as he sat on the bed. "There are a few things we have to work out, like what I expect from you." Sara did not acknowledge him in any way but continued to brush her long hair. "Ah, so we are going to be childish, are we? Fine, I'll do the talking."

"There's a big surprise," she said softly. She knew he heard her. There was nothing wrong with his hearing.

"At precisely six o'clock, I will be back in here to escort you downstairs. You will be ready to receive guests with me. What I want from you is anything you might feel from the people in the room. I don't care how mundane you feel it is. I want to know about it. You feed me the information through telepathy, and none will be the wiser. Any questions?" She didn't answer him. "No? Fine. I'll see you in two hours." He turned and left.

~~~

Minutes after he left her to her bath, Mel contacted her.

"Hello, little warrior. Tonight is your big date, is it not? I so wish I could see you in your gown in person."

"You know it's not a date. Something's wrong. What's the matter? You never contact me this time of day." She suddenly had visions of Sherman finding out where his mate was and killing everyone on site.

"Everything is fine. I'm fine. I left the nursing home yesterday. I'm now in Molavonta. I'm safe. I've sealed myself in my high tower and will stay here until I'm able to come to you. I'll be where you are in two days." Sara relaxed a little but tensed at her next words. *"Sara, you will need to make time to talk with me. It is imperative that we get things in order before Sherman finds out that I'm back in the Kingdom of Molavonta again. Things need to be finalized, you understand me?"*

"Yes, I understand." Sara did not like her tone or what she was saying. But she was her queen.

"I will see you on Sunday at sunset then. I want you not to worry, little one. I'm very strong now. You've done well. Have fun this evening and be the belle of the ball." The connection closed with a mental hug from Mel. Sara couldn't help but smile at the feeling it evoked in her heart.

~~~

At ten to six, just as Aaron was heading up the stairs to get Sara, Duncan came from the kitchen with a message for him.

"The little miss called. It seems she's having some difficulty with her clothing. She asks that you would please give her a few minutes, and she will be down shortly."

"What kind of clothing problems? She's wearing her dress, isn't she? Please tell me it's not her flight clothes? That would be just like her, to piss me off, you know?" He thought that if she did come down in her uniform, it would be no less than he deserved. He had been a rude, overbearing ass to her all day.

"I'm sure I don't know, my lord. She said that she will be down, for you not to get your, I believe she called them 'panties' in a twist and start pounding on the door. She said that it would not make it any easier for her to figure things out." Aaron was sure there was more to what Duncan was telling him but decided that he would let it go.

At twelve after the hour, Aaron started up the stairs to get her. Guests would be arriving soon, and he wanted her beside him. In what capacity, he just wasn't sure yet.

The mistress from this afternoon told him he must decide if he wanted her for his mate, that she needed to get Sara together with someone who would be a partner to her for life. She could just as easily sever that potential bond before it was too late for either of them if he did not want her. Did he? He was not any closer to knowing the answer to that than he had been earlier.

Aaron heard her speaking before he saw her, which was a good thing, or he may have fallen on his face without the extra few seconds of warning. As it was, he gripped hard on the banister and watched as she made her way down the long, winding staircase, her heels clicking on the stone steps.

"I know, I know, I'm late, but I had trouble with this bra thingy. A torture device, if you ask me. It has twenty-two eyehooks up the front. And since I didn't try it on in the shop, I wasn't sure how to put it on." As she spoke, her arms moved and made her breasts move as well. He could feel the drool forming on his tongue. "Then if that isn't bad enough, it's mashing my entire bosom into a puffed up mass to have it spill out of the flippin' thing. Once I got the stupid thing on, I realized I needed to take it off again. Have you ever tried to pull on stockings with boobs in your face? Not possible, let me warn you. Of course, they aren't the regular pantyhose either. Oh no, they're these sheer socks that pull up to the mid-thigh. How I'm expected to keep them up all night is beyond me! Then back into the iron maiden thing. It's not that I don't like the dress and shoes, but just look at these things. Why one wants to walk on their toes like this all night is beyond stupid."

Sara had been walking down the grand staircase as she ranted. Aaron watched each step she took, looking at whatever she had been going on about at the time; bosom, chest exposure, legs. Now she stood before him, one step up so that they were eye level. She was looking at him expectantly while waiting for him to make a comment about the state of her shoes she was now showing him—or some other nonsense; he simply could not remember what she had been saying. She was his. All his, and he needed to stake his claim right now.

When she dropped the hem of the dress and stood up, he reached out and cupped his hand behind her neck, pulling her into his embrace, into his kiss. *Mine,* was all he thought before he covered his mouth with hers and devoured her.

Aaron tasted her lips, pulling the lower one into his mouth, and then ran his tongue along the seam, requesting permission to enter. She leaned into him and allowed him in.

"*Aaron, please,*" she begged, whispering desperately through his mind. He answered her by pulling her tighter against him, slipping his thigh between her legs, and cupping her ass with his other hand and pulling her harder against his cock. Need was a living, breathing thing between them now, and it was not going to be denied, he thought.

Neither seemed to realize nor care that there were people standing around them in the entrance hall, their sudden need overpowering all reason. When Colin cleared his throat for the third time, Aaron reluctantly pulled away but did not release Sara.

"Shall we turn everyone away, or can you two hold off until everyone is gone? Just say the word, and I'll get rid of everyone who comes to the door." Aaron turned to look at his best friend and saw his cocky grin. He smiled when Colin winked at Sara.

Aaron turned back to look at the woman in his arms, who was currently turning several shades of red from her embarrassment at getting caught practically making love on the stairs. He had no doubt whatsoever that that would have been where they would have ended up had they not been interrupted.

"No, Mr. Larimore, that won't be necessary." She blushed deeper when Aaron pulled her tighter in his arms. "I don't know what came over me. I must have slipped. Yes, that's it. Thank you, Mr. Mac…Aaron, for catching me. I'm okay now. Let's get this over with, shall we?"

Before she could take a step away from him, he pulled her back into his arms and kissed her again. "Make no mistake, Sara, love, you did not fall, and we are going to finish this tonight." He kissed her again and then pulled away from her with a great deal of reluctance.

When the first guests arrived, Sara had not left his side, not that she could have, as he had not let go of her hand once since they had kissed on the stairs. She was relaying him information automatically and without much thought as to what she was telling him. Finally, he couldn't take it anymore and laughed.

"When I said to tell me everything, love, I thought you'd just send me snippets of information, not life stories." Sara had just finished telling Aaron about a woman's, Abby Allen's, one-sided conversation with herself about her and her mate's horrible experience just that evening and the human they had encountered. The human had touched Abby, and she was sure that she smelled just like the human, all scented up with cheap perfume and body odor. Sara had been giving Aaron her opinions right along with the story.

"I'm sorry. I know you said everything, but I'm sure you didn't mean that mundane," she groused at him.

"No, probably not." He brought her hand to his mouth and kissed the back of it. He watched as her pupils dilated. *"But it is fun to watch and hear you get all flustered."*

No one could guess the couple was talking to each other.

They likely just assumed that Sara was told to be silent, and she was obeying. She was nothing more than a snack for the master anyway, and a very nice-looking snack at that.

"I'm not flustered, thank you very much. I'm reflective."

"Oh, and what's the difference? Because I have to tell you, I've never been more flustered in my life. All I can think about doing right now is throwing you against the nearest wall, lifting your dress, and seeing what other delights you have under there." He pulled her closer to him and nipped at her neck. *"You never told me about what your panties are like. I know about your stockings, which I will take great delight in removing from you one leg at a time, rolling them down, inch by incredible inch, kissing the exposed skin as I go. Then there are those enticing twenty-two eyehooks that I can't wait to open one at a time until your breasts spill out into my hands and my mouth. Oh, sweetheart, I want to suckle on your nipples until you come."*

"Oh my," she whispered to him breathlessly.

"Yes, my dear, 'oh my' about covers it for now."

Aaron could not wait to have her beneath him, riding him, naked with him, and after the last two hours of people falling at his feet, he wanted to taste her in the worst way. He was not waiting any longer, damn it. He began making his way to the nearest room with a door and a lock. His strides made short work of the otherwise long trek across the grand hall, dragging her right along with him. When they got to the powder room just off the main hall, he pulled her in behind him and shut the door. He jerked her body to his and was kissing her before she could speak, much less protest.

God, he wanted her. It was several seconds of heavy breathing and heated kisses later when he heard the door lock engage. He pulled back from her and grinned. "Good girl," he said before he lifted her up by her bottom, sat her on the vanity of the small room, and positioned himself between her legs. When she hooked her ankles together behind him and around his hips, he nearly cried with relief. But kissing her was no longer enough.

No, not nearly enough at all.

"Sara, I want you now. I need to be inside of you. But this isn't the time or the place to make love to you. Let me taste of you, baby, please?"

Without waiting for a reply, he dropped down to the toilet seat, pulled her forward to the edge of the sink, and began lifting the dress up her legs. He watched every inch he exposed of her legs, knowing that paradise was just a foot or two away. When he ran his hand up her thigh and encountered her skin left bare by the top of her stockings, he nearly whimpered with his need to touch more of her. His hands traveled farther, cupping her bared ass cheeks in each hand, pulling her to him. He could smell her; her juices were already soaking her panties through. He could almost taste the nectar that was his and his alone. He didn't go for seduction. He couldn't, his need, their need, was too high. He bit through the tiny scrap of lace and ripped it away. *Finally,* he thought, what he wanted, her. Aaron tilted her hips, leaned his head forward, and took his first taste of her creamy, wet flesh.

"Please, Aaron…." she begged him.

"Soon, baby, soon. I want you to come for me. Let me feel you come against my mouth. I want to taste your cum. Now, Sara, now—come for me!"

With a scream tearing from deep in her throat, she came hard, nearly squeezing Aaron's head off from the tightening of her legs around it. He kept tasting her and taking her rich cream into his body until she fell back against the mirror over the sink. He stood up, pulling his pants open as he did, and his erection jumped forward toward her.

"Sara, touch me, touch me now." As she reached out for his cock, he took her hand in his and wrapped it around his hard shaft, showing her what he needed for her to do. The moment her hot hand touched his cock, he knew that he couldn't last. He moved against her with each downward stroke of her hand, kissing her deeply and thinking about what it was going to feel like once it was his cock inside of her deliciously hot pussy. He began sending her mental pictures of what they were going to do once he got her alone in his bed.

As she started sending him her own mental pictures of her need, she moved her mouth down his jaw just below the collar of his shirt and bit. His body jerked as her teeth, while not breaking skin, clamped down on the vein in his throat. That was all it took. His fangs, already elongated from his need for her, burst forward, and he struck quickly, opening the vein at her creamy neck, and came, ejaculating in her hand while her hot blood filled his mouth. When he pulled hard on her throat with his mouth, sucking more of her richness into him, she came, and with each draw from her vein, Sara came again and again until she fainted dead away from the intense pleasure.

She was out only a few seconds, but it was long enough for him to worry he might have hurt her in some way.

"Are you all right, love?"

"No, I don't think I'll ever be right again. That was incredible! I never knew...I mean, I'd heard, but...I...did you...I mean, I know you, you know...but did you, you know...?"

Aaron burst out laughing. He didn't think he had ever been so happy. "Yes, sweetheart, I did. And yes, that was the most incredible experience of my life as well. I can't wait to take you to my bed and experience so many more incredible things with you."

"Now?" She leaned forward to kiss him as she asked.

"As much as I'd like to, Sara, we have a house full of guests, most of which will still need to see me before sunrise. Come with me, and let's get this over with so we can be alone."

Aaron pulled away from her reluctantly and began to straighten her and himself up. He didn't know how to hide the stain that was now down the front of his shirt and her dress, but Sara simply swiped her hand down over the area, and they were both as pristine as when they'd come into the little bathroom, if not a little more relaxed with each other.

CHAPTER FIFTEEN

Aaron and Sara had become quite the topic of conversation once they returned from the powder room. Every vampire in the room could smell Sara all over the master. There was also much speculation on what she was exactly.

"This lady is afraid you'll ask for more money. Good heavens! You can take that much from each of your people?"

Sara had gotten much better at filtering out the information before she fed it to him, she thought. She was not sending him as much useless stuff and more tidbits of thoughts they were having.

"I only take a percentage of what they make. It all goes into a fund for the alliance, minus two percent for my expenses. Why, how much are you talking about?" Sara stood by Aaron and watched yet another vamp pledge their solidarity to him.

"She was giving the other master forty percent of their total income from their businesses. Sheesh. And the amount came to sixty thousand per year. Sixty thousand? Are you kidding me?" Sara was amazed at the amount, especially when she considered there were times when she would go for days without food in order to pay her meager bills.

"We live a very long time, so we can invest in many successful business ventures over the years. Plus, most of us have several homes, so rent and food are not a problem, nor is electric and heating, as we have excellent eyesight, even at night, and have no need for heat or cooling. The money also pays for security and medical help. A lot of

these vamps have daywalkers as help and protection. When they get hurt or injured, it's safer for us if they see a doctor of our choice. Then there are the orphans of murdered vampires. In order to care for them, we pay others to take them in and raise them. While children are rare, the ones we manage to have are very precious to us."

"So the money paid to you stays within your realm. That's good." After a few seconds, she asked, *"Who in this room would be using very strong magic?"*

"Vampires don't have magic."

She looked at him to see if he was joking. He didn't appear to be. *"Well, of course, you do, don't be stupid. Someone is using a great deal of...I have to check something out. Will you stay here?"* She was just moving away from him when she realized where the magic may be coming from.

"Where are you going? Stay here with me, please." He was not in a position to follow her, as he was talking with a group of men who thought it might be a good idea to open their own bank and blood bank.

"I have to see about something. I can feel a magic that I've only felt once before. Let me see if I'm right or not. I'll be all right. I just want to check on something."

Sara moved her way to the front of the room, toward the great entrance hall. She gently reached for the people she had been asked to protect, searching for them in the large ballroom and beyond. April and Demetrius were...ewww, were having sex in the dark corner of another room just off the main hall. Duncan was in his kitchen. And Colin...was right in front of her.

"So, Mr. Colin, Aaron sent you after me, did he?" She folded her arms across her chest, careful not to pop her boobs out of the top of her dress.

"Yes, mistress. He seems to think you might get yourself into all kinds of mischief if he isn't around to curb you. Imagine that."

She laughed when he mimicked her stance. Colin looked very nice in his tux with tails, filling it out in all the right places.

Not as good as Aaron, but good nonetheless. She was also aware of the reason for the tails. He was hiding several blades and a handgun up under the back of the jacket.

"He's probably right. Something is wrong. There's a being here that's using dark magic. I need your help. Will you trust me?"

"Yes." He answered her without hesitation.

"I believe Aaron's in danger." He turned away and started toward Aaron. "No, don't go to him. I promise you nothing will happen to him, but I do want to catch the corrupt who dares to threaten his life. He's coming to the door as we speak, and he has five men with him. Can you get some men who you know are loyal to your master and have them follow the newcomers? Wait for my signal. When I'm ready, I'll need you to apprehend them as soon as I let you know who they are." She continued toward the front door. Colin followed.

"I'm at your service, My Lady. Just tell me how I'll know what they look like." As he spoke, he reached behind his jacket and pulled out a short, jeweled dagger. Turning it handle first, he handed it to her. "It's silver on the tip, and the handle will open like this." He pushed on a green jewel, probably an emerald, and a long, thin spike shot from the opposite end. "And there you go."

"Great, thank you. I'll send you a mental picture and their location. Be careful, Mr. Colin. They carry silver blades."

"Always, My Lady. We will await your signal." That was the second time he had called her that. She would have to ask him about it when this was over, she thought. With a small bow, he started back into the large ballroom.

"*Oh, and Mr. Colin, don't bite them anywhere. It will prove to be fatal to anyone who does,*" she sent to him telepathically.

Sara backed deep into a hidden corner and waited. She felt Sherman enter the mansion the moment he crossed the threshold. His power base had weakened somewhat, she realized. Now that he was in the house proper, he was as weak as a normal human. When she'd covered the house in a protective shell, she never would have thought it would be Mel's mate who would test its strength. Anyone who entered with ill intent would be stripped of their magic, and Sherman was nothing but ill will.

Sara followed rather than attacked. She could not read his mind, and if she stepped in too soon, she would lose her advantage of being able to hide herself from him until she figured out what he wanted by coming there.

As soon as she realized who the guards were, she sent the information to Colin. She was surprised to find Marcus Freely among them. A careful scan of his mind revealed much, a lot more than she could have hoped for. He and the others were not there of their own free will, but by force. She touched him to see if he would talk to her, explain; she thought he would never shut up. He was worried about his family, and he had good reason. They were being held hostage and would be murdered if he and the others didn't help slay the new Master of the Realm.

Marcus was the Master of the Guard in Molavonta. He had also been the one who had recruited her for the queen's personal guard. He was a loyal and trusted friend. If he thought Sherman would murder his family if he did not cooperate, then she had to help him.

"*You give me your word, Marcus. Give me your word that you'll lay down your sword and not raise it against me and mine. You do this, and I'll make sure your family is safe.*"

"*You have it. And my sword, if I live,*" he promised her.

"*You will live.*" She would make sure that he did. "*You'll need to trust me. I have a plan. It's risky, but it'll work if you trust me. Do you?*"

"*With my life and that of my family, I give you my trust, Sara.*" She heard the promise in his voice. "*The men, my men, they're all here....*"

"*I know, my friend. I'll make sure you're all safe. I promise you.*"

Sara had to wait until she heard from Colin. She needed to make sure he had the other four men before she could make her move. But when Sherman moved closer to Aaron, she leapt forward to intercede.

As she neared the two men, Marcus and Sherman neither felt nor heard her approach. It was not until she had the jeweled knife at Sherman's throat that she let her shield down and her magic free.

"Hello, Shermie," she whispered in his ear. "What brings you to a vampire dinner? Hopefully, you're volunteering to be the main course."

Sherman jerked against her hold on him. She was physically and magically more fit than him, so he could not shake her loose. She could feel his anger roll off him. It made her smile that she finally had the upper hand when dealing with him.

"Bitch! My name is Sherman, your master. You would do well to remember that in the future," he hissed at her.

"Aaron." She jerked tighter on Sherman when she felt him try to lunge at Aaron. "Step away from the lunatic, if you please? He can't use his magic here, but he did bring you a little gift."

"Sara, what's going on?" Aaron asked.

"He's here to kill you. Aren't you, Shermie?" She pushed the blade deeper into his neck. She could not draw blood because of his high position in the kingdom, but she wanted to.

"I don't know what you are talking about," Sherman sputtered. "You were always a bit unstable, and this just proves it. Don't listen to her, Aaron. I've come here to offer you any assistance you might need as the new master. I'll take this...person back to Molavonta so that she can stand trial. My kingdom has been looking for her for years. She murdered my dear mate, you know?"

"Step back, Aaron." She could see by the look on Aaron's face he was shocked about what Sherman had said, but right now, she had enough to worry about other than what he may think of her.

"You'll see what I'm talking about."

Aaron finally took one step back, then two more. He looked down at what the man had in his hands and along the front of his tux. He could see now that Sherman was covered in long, thin, sharp needles. Without a doubt, Sara thought, they were pure silver.

"Oh, Sara. Don't you know how the game is played?" He was smirking. She didn't have to see his face to realize that. His voice dripped with venom and hatred. "You think for one moment you can stop me? Harm me? I think not. For now, even as I stand here, my men are rallying behind me to do my bidding."

She had felt Colin move up just to her left. "You think so, Shermie? Mr. Colin, did you see any of his men?"

"Yeah, love, I'm here. And the only 'troops' we found was this group of children." She felt the man she held jerk at Colin's voice. He had absolutely believed he would be victorious in killing Aaron.

Colin and four other of his men were holding a man each who looked like they'd put up a good fight. The four captives were a part of the lesser guard, younger men without much experience. Colin walked up to Marcus, pulled him hard against his chest, and put his dirk to his throat.

"You shouldna bring such babies to a mons fight. Dinna have ta break a sweat to bring'em down, no fun in that."

Sara smiled to herself. Colin's accent got just a little heavier when he was mad, she thought facetiously. She would have to remember that.

"Are these your troops, Shermie? A bedraggled group, to be sure." She looked at the men Colin's men were holding. They were covered in dirt and presumably their own blood. The vampires that had helped subdue them were as pristine as when they had left to help apprehend them.

"I swear if you call me that disgusting name once more, I will—"

"You'll what?" she asked him. "Right now, you are at my command. You will demand nothing, you understand, you worthless piece of shit?" He had dared to try and hurt what she now considered hers. Not bloody likely.

"I'm royalty. I command you," he practically spit at her. "You will bow before me, you insolent human. I demand that you set me free."

Sara couldn't help it. Sara laughed at him.

Aaron clearing his throat, brought her back to the situation at hand. "You've come into my home to kill me, Shermie. If so, then Sara's correct…you have no rights as far as I'm concerned. What did you hope to gain by killing me, I wonder?"

Sherman said nothing, but Sara wasn't finished. She'd promised to save Marcus and needed to make that work for him and the men he commanded.

"Marcus, you have wounded me. You've come into my master's home like this, thinking to draw first blood. The rules of war demand a forfeit, a forfeit of a life. As this is the home of MacManus, he is the one to be satisfied." She turned to Aaron and prayed reverently that this worked. "How many will it be, Mr. MacManus?"

"*One*," she whispered through his mind. She hoped that he would not ask questions. But she didn't want to take the chance of saying more to him in case Sherman could hear them. "Mr. MacManus? You have the rights of war that govern the Kingdom of Molavonta, the castle keep and home to the Queen of Magic. Your home has been compromised by these men," Sara explained to him when he didn't answer. "You must choose the amount you feel is owed to you."

When he looked at her, she gave him the tiniest shake of her head. Just one, she thought to herself, please just one.

"Colin, I would say one, what say you?" Aaron asked Colin. Neither man looked too confused, for which she was grateful.

"Aye, that sounds about right. We got the pleasure of beating the crap outta these buggers, so one should suffice."

Sara smiled again when Colin gave Marcus a good shake. Poor Marcus, she hoped he lived through Colin's manhandling. She knew from experience he was a vigorous shaker.

"Marcus, as Master of the Guard, you choose." She hoped Marcus would be brave. She didn't want to do this, but it was the only way. "Which man will you give over?"

"Sara, you cannot ask this of me to give up the life of one of my men. No, not you, I cannot believe it of you. I won't," he said.

"I am no longer the queen's guard, so I no longer play by her rules. Pick. I don't have all night. The sun will rise soon, and my lord will need to seek his bed. Now pick one man to die," she snapped at him.

Marcus turned to the man next to him. "Jacob...?" For several tense filled moments, not a sound was made.

Jacob Donaldson was perhaps the youngest man in the group but the most loyal to his queen, Sara knew. He was at most twenty-five, while the others were only a couple of years older if that.

Jacob stepped forward to take the blow that would end his life. Her sweep of his mind made her respect the young man all the more.

"Yes, sir," he said. His lips wavered as he held his chin up in a show of bravery.

"Tell my wife and family that I love them very much and will see them on the other side." Marcus turned back to Sara, resignation heavy on his face. "Me, Sara, I pick me to pay the forfeit."

The small group surrounding them stiffened in surprise. They had all thought that young Jacob was his choice. Sara shoved Sherman to the floor and stepped over his inert body to reach where Marcus now stood alone.

"So be it. May the queen honor your death, Marcus Freely, Master of Arms of the queen's Royal Guard." Sara lashed out with her own blade and slit the older man's throat with a clean slice. As he dropped to the floor, blood poured from the wound and spread out before the men, pooling beneath him in an expanding puddle.

Not a sound was made for a good thirty seconds, then in a voice devoid of any emotion, Sara said to the man lying on the floor next to her friend, "It's a shame that I can't kill you as well, you son of a bitch. But as you did not succeed in your quest to kill my lord, then I must let you go by rules of your kind. However, heed this." She knelt down to him. "When we next meet, I'll not be as kind as I was to the dead man before you. Your death will be a pleasure, long and hard. I will make you suffer dearly for what you've taken from me." With a mental and physical push, he was tossed across the room a good ten feet.

"You've not heard the end of this, you fucking whore," Sherman said to her as he scrambled to his feet. "You think you bested me this time, but when we do meet again, I will be the one doing the killing. You won't be able to hold my magic from me. Then we'll see just who is the stronger of the two of us."

Sherman gathered himself up and left the house, abandoning the men he brought with him to be dealt with as the Master of the Realm wished.

CHAPTER SIXTEEN

"Sara, there's a dead man on my floor." Aaron sounded calm, even to himself. "What do you propose we do about it?"

She had just killed a man in cold blood, sliced him while he stood in front of them and killed him. Killing men who were here for murder of their own free will was one thing, but this man had done nothing wrong but been a part of a hired force.

"Nothing yet. I want to make sure Sherman is well and truly gone first." She dropped completely to the floor from her knees, landing in the blood surrounding Marcus. Aaron believed her to be waiting for the man to die. He was reasonably sure Marcus was dead; there was too much blood for him to be otherwise.

"Colin. Colin!"

Colin turned to look at Sara, shock at what he had seen her do evident on his face, Aaron noticed. Everyone was shocked.

"Have these men taken to a cell. Colin! Are you listening? Have these men taken to a holding cell!" she snapped. Her voice was exhausted sounding.

"Yes," Colin said with a shake of his head. "Daniel, Scott, please take them below and lock them in a cell."

Colin moved to do her bidding. Aaron wondered if Colin had even noticed that he had not asked his master for permission.

After a minute or two, Sara touched Marcus. "Wake up, Marcus, you've been lazing about long enough." Aaron watched as she gave the dead man another hard poke to the ribs. "Get up, you lazy bastard. We have things to do."

Aaron started to move forward, to pick her up and away from the body. He was sure that killing this man had pushed her over the edge of reason. When Marcus rolled over and looked up at Sara with tears in his eyes, Aaron was shocked once again, more so by the man's statement than by the fact that he was not dead.

"You saved me," Marcus told her.

"Of course, I did. I said I would, didn't I? Now get up. You're making the vamps nervous. They believe I murdered you."

"He's not dead." Colin turned to look at Aaron. "You dinna kill the mon. But the blood, all that blood. I saw you slice his throat. I donna understand."

Neither did Aaron, actually, but he waited to see what she had to say.

"I couldn't kill anyone in cold blood, but I thank you for having such a high opinion of me and thinking that I could." She shrugged as if it mattered little. "When I found him among the guards, I found out he was here against his will. As are those men you took below. Sherman has their families. He's holding them captive until he succeeded in killing you, Aaron. He told me what was happening and asked that I save his family."

"My family!" Marcus jumped from the floor and toward the doors when Sara's voice stopped him.

"The queen has your family with her in the high tower of Molavonta Keep. They are all there, including your mother and that stupid dog of yours. The other men's families are there as well, safe and sound."

The man staggered slightly, and Aaron leaped forward to grab him before he fell to the floor. He gently sat him down and watched the man's tears flow freely.

"The queen is sending someone to get you, and you will be reunited with them as soon as possible. The other men will need to stay here, at least for a few days. If that's all right with you?" She had turned toward Aaron as she spoke.

Aaron looked at her. Sara was pale, and her skin was clammy-looking. Then he noticed that her hands were trembling. When she noticed him staring, she put her hands in her lap and held them together.

"Oh, so now you want to involve me? How nice," Aaron growled. He was annoyed. No, he was pissed at her. "You planned this all without as much as a word to me? Did it occur to you that I may have been killed for real had I embraced that, that mad man? That anyone in this room may have attacked you, or any other person standing here when they saw you 'pretend' to take that man's life? This blood...." He looked down at the now clean floor. He looked up at her, confused when she stood up. "Sara?"

"I didn't cut him. My knife is still upstairs in my bag. You saw what I wanted you to see," she said, and then staggered before she fell to the floor in a heap again. Aaron immediately went to her aid. She was weak; he could feel it when he touched her.

"And the others? What if they had attacked you? How would you have handled the two hundred vampires that also saw all this blood? You can barely stand now."

"No one in this room knew what she was doing. No one saw anything at all, save those of you who were involved." This voice came from just behind Aaron. He turned to see who was speaking and found himself looking at the woman from his bedroom. Had that only been yesterday afternoon? "She'll need juice, lots of juice. Using that much magic takes a great deal of energy."

"Someone go to the kitchen and have Duncan make her what he has that's fast," Aaron told the person next to him. "If he doesn't have anything, send someone who can move quickly to get it for her. Tell him to bring whatever he has right now, quickly, please."

As a younger vamp took off into the kitchen, Aaron looked around the room and saw that Mel was correct. Everyone was mingling and talking as if nothing was out of the ordinary. In fact, other than the occasional glance their way, no one seemed to be paying the slightest bit of attention to them.

"How is that possible?" he asked Mel as she moved closer to the group.

"I told you she was very strong yesterday. Sara made everyone standing here believe that she'd killed Marcus, the knife slicing through him, spilling his blood on the floor. Also, the house itself has been held. Whatever wasn't a vampire, their magic was taken from them and left at the door. So as soon as Sherman entered, he was magically powerless against her."

Aaron looked down at the woman in his arms. "That still doesn't explain why I wasn't warned. I could have helped you. I should have helped you." He handed her the juice off the tray Duncan had brought in. He had perhaps nine full glasses of juice there, varying in colors and smells.

"I needed you to believe he was harmless," Sara said after draining the first glass. "Had I given you a warning, let you know what he was up to, he would have read that in you and acted accordingly. He would have simply thrown himself against you at the first opportunity."

Aaron handed her a second glass, and she drained it as she had the first. He looked around the room again. No one was the wiser. But he was no less pissed about the whole thing. She could have been hurt or killed. As his mate, it was his job to protect her, not the other way around. As soon as possible, they were going to have to set up some guidelines. Not rules, she would not follow rules, but guidelines she may.

"So you have made your decision then. Good choice, Master of the Realm. But I wouldn't count on the guidelines either if I were you," Mel said with a laugh.

"Choice? Guidelines? What are you talking about? Come to think of it, how do you two know each other?" Sara struggled to stand, and he held her still. He liked holding her, regardless of how mad he was at her.

"Lie still. You're still weak. Here, drink another glass of this yellow stuff. Mel came to my room today…well, yesterday…and we had a long talk. You and I will talk about it later."

Aaron should have known better. He felt her trample through his mind like a steamroller. Had it been physical instead of a mental search, he would have bruises all over his head. And from the way she was looking at him right now, he may end up with them anyway.

"You've decided to keep me? Well, how fucking nice for you, you arrogant ass. Was I going to get a choice in this? No, I can see that it didn't occur to you. Either of you, for that matter. How could you?" She was crying. He had made her cry again, damn it. She turned to Mel. "And you, what right do you have making any choices for me? You hoped that I would, what, roll over and do what you say?" She struggled out of his arms as she yelled at Mel, but rather than hurt her, he let her go. "Oh my God — and the queen? You've decided that I would be the queen, too? How dare you? How dare either of you?"

"I told you that I've made decisions," Melody snapped at her. "I told you that they affected you. If I hadn't done this, you would still be floundering about using only a small part of what you are. I helped you."

Aaron took a step back. He could feel the anger rolling heavily off both women. He had learned many, many years ago, never to step between women when they fought. They fought by their own rules, and they were not always…nice about it.

"Helped me? Are you insane? What happens to you? Do you just fade away again? End up in some field while I deal with everything again?" Sara looked at the door when no one answered her. "And what about Sherman? Huh? You think he'll just say, 'Oh good, you're queen now. You go right ahead. I'll be seeing you around?' Fuck you!"

"Sara, she was only trying to help," Aaron said. "She couldn't go on. You know as well as anyone why she can't."

He knew the queen's plan for him and Sara; they were to rule her kingdom together. While he did not necessarily agree with her methods, he was at least willing to acknowledge that the continuation of the lineage was vital.

"You knew about all of this? Before us...before the bathroom?" she asked him, hurt in her voice. "You bit me!"

"You wanted that as much as I did," he snapped. "You are not going to lay that one on me alone. And yes, I knew before you came downstairs tonight, so what? It makes no difference now; you are mine, my mate for all eternity."

He regretted saying it the moment it left his mouth. Not the words, no, never that, but his timing could have been a tad better, he thought.

There was a sudden tightening in the room as if it somehow grew bigger than the space allowed. No one moved. No one dared to. When Aaron started to speak again, Sara held up her hand to silence him. He was too stunned by the move to ignore it. After several tension-filled seconds, Sara spoke to them.

"I want you both to never contact me again. I am not going to be queen, nor am I going to be a mate to you or anyone else. Period. I hate you both for what you've presumed to think for me, the decisions you've made for me, and the secrets you kept from me. Stay away from me."

Sara stood again and took a look around the room. Then she turned on her heel and ran from the room, toward the front entrance hall, and out into the late evening night.

"Sara! Sara, come back here this minute!" He flashed himself forward, only to be stopped suddenly by a wall. Her magic, he thought. Her magic was working against him rather than for him now.

CHAPTER SEVENTEEN

After everyone had paid homage to Aaron and left the mansion long before sunrise, the remaining people adjourned to the massive living room to go over the strange events of the evening. The coziness of the room was in complete contrast to the mood of the people in it. The Carlovettis were very worried about Sara; she was becoming very important to them and wondered what she would do now.

Colin was still marveling at the way she made them all believe she had killed a man. He was also amazed at how she took charge and did what needed to be done without a second's hesitation or any lack of confidence.

Mel was mad, thinking that Sara was being extremely selfish about the whole thing. She would rule all of the magical elements of the world. Why should she not want that?

Aaron was angry as well, but he was not sure at whom he should be the maddest at, Sara for leaving without letting him explain, Mel for not allowing him to explain things to her in his own way, or himself for not telling her anything. No, he mused, he was mad at himself most of all. He should have trusted her; he should have told her what he suspected from the beginning... that she was his mate, his partner. More than that, he should have treated her like one.

"Do you have any idea what level of power was required for what Sara did tonight?" Mel asked the room in general after she had been introduced to everyone.

"I know she made a believer of me — all that blood, not a drop of it real. I didn't know you could hold that many people in thrall. Did you, Aaron?" Colin turned to his friend and master.

"She didn't, not really. You see, that's what I'm talking about," Mel went on to clarify. "She held each vampire in a state of separate thrall, unique to each one of them."

Aaron didn't really care how she did it. He just wanted to bring her back so he could tell her how sorry he was.

"I don't understand. What do you mean separate thrall?" Colin asked her.

"Each vampire has unique abilities of their own, right? Colin, you can read a person's lies, scan their body for hidden objects and whatever else they may be hiding. Demetrius, even for your age, you're a remarkably strong and talented telepath. Aaron, you have a great many talents. Some of them from age, others from practice." Mel started to pace the room as she spoke. Aaron noticed that Sara did the same thing. "You see, each of your minds works differently with your magic. Sara couldn't just rely on one bit of magic to keep others from becoming involved. She needed to take each one of your abilities and use them against you. No one saw or heard what she didn't want them to. She didn't get that from me. She's using power well beyond what I've given her. Beyond anything I've ever seen. She isn't just a Keeper like me; she is more than me in some ways."

"What are you saying? Are you saying Sara is not human, that she is a different species than any of us?" Aaron finally asked.

"Is she tattooed with any markings?" Mel asked. "Anything more than this?" She showed everyone her tattoo as the Queen of Magick. Looking almost like a photograph, the tattoo depicted a half-moon in light blue-grayish tones with the sun, a bright yellow, rising from it. Beneath the sun and moon stood a tree in different seasons of the year: spring with tiny buds on strong limbs; summer with full, dark-green leaves straining toward the heavens; fall with blended leaves of orange and red; winter with bare limbs. "Sara's would be smaller and without color...or very little color...maybe just shades of gray."

No one had seen any marking at all on her, other than the bruises the first days she was at the mansion.

~~~

It was four days before Sara contacted anyone—four long and miserable days without a word to anyone in the mansion as to where she was, what she was doing, or if she would forgive them. Mel tried to contact Sara mentally, but she had shut her out as tightly as if she no longer existed. Aaron used a more modern method, the phone, but had as little success as Mel did.

When she finally made contact, it was to phone the Carlovettis. "Mr. Carlovetti, it's Sara Temple. I was wondering if I could talk with you, please?"

Sara had been staying at the hotel out on Route Forty. It was okay as far as hotels went. It was clean and was cooler than it was outdoors. Summers in Ohio were abhorrent.

"Sara, thank God! Are you all right? We've been so worried about you. Yes, yes, of course, any time. Just let me know where to meet you."

"Now is fine," she told him. "That is if you have the time. But if you try to contact anyone else, I'll know, and I'll end this conversation immediately, all right?"

Sara had been trying to work up the nerve to call the Carlovettis for two days. She didn't want to get them into trouble with their master, but she was running low on funds. All her extra cash was hidden in her van, which was currently residing at the mansion.

"I wasn't going to contact anyone. I believe what they did was wrong to a point. Sara, you need to contact Aaron. He's suffering badly."

"Let him." Sara's heart took a hard knock at the thought of him suffering. But damn it, she was tired of everyone trying to tell her what she needed.

"I was wondering if I am still able to work for your company? I need a job and some money. I wouldn't do anything to jeopardize you or your company, so I will understand completely if you say no."

If he said no, which she hoped he would not, she would have to move to Columbus and get a job. Now that Mel had shown up, there was no reason to hide any longer. Well, except for the High Council of Magick and the sanction to have her put to death—minor details. Hopefully, with Mel found, Sara would no longer be hunted by them.

Demetrius was silent for a long few minutes. So long, in fact, that she knew for sure, he was going to turn her down. She was about to tell him to forget it when he answered her.

"Yes, you have a job, so long as you want it. Sara, I'll keep your employment quiet for as long as I can. Because we both know as soon as Aaron finds out you're working again, he'll want to talk to you. And if he does, then I'll have to comply so long as you're working for me when he finds out."

"I understand, and I appreciate that. Thank you."

Demetrius had just told her that if Aaron found out, she needed to be gone before he had to make her go see him.

"I won't let you down. I swear." She wouldn't either.

"I know you won't, Sara. I'll see you tomorrow then." He hung up first. She thought he sounded hurt.

Another week passed. Sara flew out early every evening and returned late the next afternoon, well after the highest part of the day was upon them. Demetrius had done well with her secret so far.

Demetrius had left her an email that first morning, asking her to be gone well before he and April got to work. He explained that he wanted to be honest with Aaron if he ever asked if Demetrius had seen her. So she made sure she was gone before sunset every evening. In exchange for him helping her out, she took home the next day's flights and made the roster up with a flight schedule.

Personal information was never exchanged on either side.

But after nearly two weeks of careful wording and planning on his part, Demetrius slipped up.

~~~

"Have you heard from Sara, Demetrius?" Aaron had been calling daily to ask the same question. He knew he wasn't going to make it much longer without feeding. Eleven days was a very long time to go without sustenance, even for someone as old as he was.

"Heard from her? No, no, I've not seen her. Have you?" Demetrius answered quickly.

Too quickly. Then Aaron realized what Demetrius had said. He had not said that he hadn't heard from her, but that he hadn't seen her. Demetrius had been lying to him. No, he thought, he'd just been asking him the wrong question. He almost laughed at the cleverness of it.

"How long have you been speaking to her, Demetrius?" His voice was calm and resigned. Sara must know that he was asking about her, but apparently, she didn't care to see him.

"Since right after the party. She contacted me the Monday afterward. And yes, I should have told you, but I couldn't...no, that's not right. I wouldn't betray her trust. Not again, not after all that she has done for me and mine."

Loyalty was something Aaron usually admired in someone, but right now, all he could think about was that Demetrius knew where she was. But he couldn't be angry, not anymore.

"Is she all right? Is she safe?" He ignored the fact that Demetrius had failed to mention that he did not trust Aaron. That much was evident in the fact that he didn't let him know about Sara's whereabouts. He had failed on so many levels with her and the others of his Kiss — his extended family. Failing to gain trust from his first bond as the master was just another on the long list of screw-ups.

"Yes, to both," Demetrius said. "Sara is flying for me

during the early evening and into the late afternoon. She's gone overnight. She needed the money, she said. I don't know where she's staying. A cab brings her to work, then picks her up, so I'm told. I know it's not far. The cab fee is less than five dollars, according to Sara, round trip."

"Yes, that explains a great deal. I need to talk to her, Demetrius. Please ask her to talk to me to see me. It's...tell her it's important that I.... We need to talk. Would you do that for me, please?"

Aaron wanted to beg her to talk to him but knew it would not do any good. If he had learned one thing about Sara Temple, it was she had a stubborn streak a mile wide and nearly just as deep.

"Yes, sir, I'll ask her. What...what punishment are you going to demand of me, sire? I'm not sorry for what I did, but I will pay the penalty. Whatever you see fit, I deserve. I just ask that you don't hurt April. She doesn't know anything about any of this. I promise you."

"Just ask her to see me, please." Aaron hung up the phone.

~~~

When Sara got to work later that night, she changed into her flight uniform. It really wasn't a bad-looking thing. The navy blue pants were tailored to fit her long legs and made of the softest cotton twill. The t-shirt was short-sleeved, with a scooped neckline of a pretty robin's egg blue. Made of silk, it clung to her curves like a second skin and felt good at the same time. The jacket, made of the same material as the pants, had three-quarter-length sleeves, two buttons with the company logo on them, and was made to just touch the top of her pants when she was standing. No name tag or other tags marred the beautiful cut and line of the clothes. Once changed, she went into the hangar.

"Demetrius wants you to wait for him to come in," Paul Potter, one of the other pilots, said as soon as he caught up with her. "He says it's important, and he needs to be face to face with you. Oh, he also said to tell you that you're safe here to stay and wait, whatever that means. Got it?"

"Yes. Thank you." This could not be good. Face to face could only mean bad things were about to hit the fan. But she would wait for him.

Nearly two hours later, Demetrius came in alone. "Thank you, Sara. I appreciate you staying to talk to me." He looked so distraught that she worried for April.

"Where's Mrs. Carlovetti? Is she all right?" She had visions of her losing the babe and nearly swept his mind to see what had happened.

"Yes, she's fine. She's coming in later. I asked her to wait until I called her before she came in."

Sara stared at him for several minutes. Demetrius wouldn't look her in the eye. Understanding was slow to come to her, but she got there eventually.

"He knows, doesn't he? He's found out, and you need to fire me, right? I'm so sorry, Mr. Carlovetti. Truly, I am. I just needed the money. I never meant to cause you problems. I'm so sorry."

Sara brushed angrily at the tears as they fell. She hated to cry. She felt it made her look weak and stupid.

"Sara, don't do that. He does know, but it's not what you think. No, you aren't fired. Nor is he asking me to do anything to you, all right? Now, let's start over, shall we? Yes, Aaron knows you're working for us again. I screwed up this morning before I left, and he caught it. All he asked was that you agree to see him. He wants to talk to you and to see you."

"No. I can't see him, Mr. Carlovetti. He hurt me, as you know. I can't...I wouldn't even know what to say to him."

He leaned back into his chair. He stared at her, saying nothing for a few minutes. "You've never let us in, April and me, have you? We've tried on several occasions to get you to call us by our first names, but you refused. You've kept us at a distance; you didn't want our friendship, so you made our relationship purely professional all these months. No matter how hard we tried, you simply shut us down. I've kept your secret for you, from my own mate and master, yet you still refuse to let me be your friend. You've never trusted that I would never hurt you or put you into a situation where you would be harmed. We know nothing about you, save what we need to know, flight plans, records, and it's all business information." Sara watched as he stood up. She had never seen him so upset before. "You know what, Sara? I feel sorry for you, more than I ever have for anyone in all my life. All you needed to do was ask, and as your friends, because that's what April and I feel like you are to us, we would have moved mountains for you. Yes. Yes, I do. I feel so sorry for you." He made to leave, but before he could walk out the door, she stopped him.

"Demetrius, I felt safer not letting people get close to me. I don't know how to have friends. I've never had one before Melody. I don't know how to be anything but what I am. I...today's my twenty-sixth birthday." She took a deep breath. "Tell Aaron... no...will you please tell Aaron that whenever it's convenient for him, I'll come to see him?" Sara left the small office and went into the now empty hangar. Instead of calling a cab to take her home, she walked the three miles back to her hotel.

CHAPTER EIGHTEEN

"His lordship is in the living room, Mistress Sara. You know the way, go on in," Duncan told her.

Sara had arrived early for her meeting with Aaron. She was not surprised by the expression on Duncan's face...she was well aware of how she looked. When she had gotten back to the hotel that evening, she had taken a good look at herself in the mirror in the bathroom and had found dark circles under her eyes. Small wonder, she thought; she had not slept well since leaving the mansion. And she had lost weight. She had never been a good judge of that sort of thing; her clothes either fit, or they didn't. She had put the dress on that she had worn to the dinner party since she could easily slip it on without bothering with the small buttons. Her hair had shocked her the most; it hung in a lank halo around her pale face without any bounce or life. Sort of like she felt.

As she made her way through the main room of the house, she didn't notice anything of her surroundings. After her talk today with Mr. Carl...no, Demetrius...she had been doing nothing but thinking about what he had said. He was right, she knew. She had never let anyone near her, not her heart or her soul. Her reasoning was that she could not get hurt if she didn't let anyone close, but that wasn't the way it worked. People tended to get in no matter what she did to keep them out.

"Hello, Sara," Aaron said from a dark corner. "Thank you for coming to see me. This won't take long. Your...home is gassed up. I also had Duncan take it in for a tune-up, and it has four new tires. I thought about replacing the thing with a motor home, but I figured you'd balk at that."

Aaron was sitting in a deep chair in the darkest part of the room. He had asked her to come late, around ten o'clock, so without the benefit of any outside light, the whole room was pitched in deep shadows. She couldn't see him, not well anyway.

"You're welcome. And thank you. Can I turn on a light or a candle? It's too dark in here." She reached out and touched him. He was starving and weak. She sat down where he had pointed: not to be polite, but because she was shocked at the extent of his weakness.

"No, I prefer it dark, thanks. I wanted to see you again before I leave. I'm going to be leaving the country. I won't be coming back. I've decided to turn over the realm to Colin to run. He'll do a good job, I believe. I've made him aware of my wishes where you're concerned. If you need anything, you can contact him, and he'll see to it that you get it. Mel is working on something to break this bond between us, so you will be free from me soon, I hope. As for the situation between you and her...I'm not sure what she is doing about the kingdom, but that is yours to resolve." He took a deep breath before he continued. "I'm sorry for everything. I've thought that if I could do it all over again, I'd change it, but we both know I wouldn't have been able to. I'm too set in my ways and all that. Do you need anything?"

She felt a stab of pain to her heart. "So you're leaving?"

While he had been telling her of his plans for her, yet again, she reflected about the man before her. She realized at the moment that she loved him. It had been coming on so slowly that she had not even realized it until he told her she would be free of him.

"Yes, I'll be honest with you, if I stay, I won't be able to stay away from you. It's better this way for both of us."

"I see. Better for both of us, or just for you?" Her temper snapped. "You know you're a pigheaded, arrogant, stubborn ass-wipe! You bring me all the way out here to give me this… what is it? Ah yes, the big 'I'm leaving for you' speech? Well, no, and hell no, you are not getting off that easy."

Every light and candle in thin the room illuminated the chair Aaron was sitting in.

Aaron suddenly leapt from the chair and was moving toward the door to the sublevels. *Oh no, he isn't*, she thought and moved to stop him. She pushed him hard against the wall near the cold fireplace. He fought her, trying to pull away.

"Oh no, you don't, big boy; look at me. I can feel your pain, your hunger. Look at me, I said." Sara cupped his face in her hands and turned him toward her. In his weakened condition, he was no match for her. She gentled her hands when she looked into his eyes. He had lost weight too, she noticed. His skin was cold and brittle. His eyes, normally so blue, were nearly devoid of color. His mouth, his lush lips, were drawn and dry.

"Don't," he begged her as he tried once again to turn away from her. She cupped his cheeks again.

"Aaron. Please, don't push me away. I'm so sorry. I…I need you." She sobbed and laid her head against his chest. She could hear his heart beating so slow under her ear. She was afraid he would push her away from him, so when his arms tightened around her, she nearly wept with happiness.

"I've missed you so much, Sara. I just wanted to see you. I…I'm so sorry, love. So sorry for everything."

"Aaron, I missed you too. Kiss me, please?"

When he leaned toward her slowly, she moaned deeply. Just the thought of his mouth on hers was sending waves of heat throughout her body. When his lips brushed against her soft ones, he moaned as well. Sara flicked her tongue out and tasted him, then pulled his lip into her mouth, nibbling on it, suckling it gently.

"Aaron, please, I need you. I want you. Please?" She pressed her body hard against his.

"Sara, I've not...I mean, I can't, we can't. I've not fed for weeks. I can't make love to you. You are...were my mate, I'm not able to feed from any other source but you, not now. I'm starving, too hungry for you to be safe around me." He pushed her away from him as he pleaded with her. "So please, baby, please leave now. You'll be safer this way."

She pulled back from his arms and looked at him. "You were going to die, weren't you?" Her laugh was harsh, even to her. "We're quite a pair, you and I." She was crying now. "Am I too late, Aaron? Have I...do you not want me anymore?"

When he didn't answer, she jerked away from him. She was nearly out the front of the house when he caught her to him. Shoving her against the door this time, he jammed his body up to hers, and while he could not get an erection, she could still tell that he wanted her, needed her.

Aaron licked his tongue down the column of her neck, nipping the tender flesh as he went. He was barely holding on to his sanity, and he did not want to hurt her. He needed to drink from her, wanted to draw her into himself and never let her go.

"Sara? Sara, baby, please?"

She didn't pull away from him but tilted her neck, giving it to him, offering all that she was to him. He licked the pulse once more and then bit down hard, tearing her skin, bruising her neck.

~~~

Mine, his mind roared. *Mine.*

He had bitten her deeper this time, drawing blood from her jugular rather than from the smaller veins in her neck. He felt her blood fill him, his cells, his lungs, and his cock. He pressed against her. Letting her feel what she was doing to him and feel his erection getting harder by the second, he ached to be inside of her. He was not going to last much longer if they stood where they were, and he knew it.

"Sara, I want you." He cupped her breast and felt the nipple pebble hard into his hand.

"Now, Aaron, please now." He sealed the small wounds at her neck with a swipe of his tongue and pulled back slightly. Her lips were swollen from his kisses. Her eyes had dilated with need. He thought she had never looked more beautiful.

"Come with me, baby." He needed to get her to a bed, his bed. He was not going to make love to her standing in the main hall where anyone would see them, at least not her first time, and not against a door.

"Oh, yes, I want to come. You come too, please...."

Aaron could almost laugh if he didn't hurt so much, ache so desperately.

"No, baby. Come with me to my bed, my lair. I need you to come to my bedroom in the sublevels. I promise we'll come as many times as you want, as many times as we possibly can. This has to be right."

Aaron picked her up, and she wrapped herself around him, her legs at his waist and offering those lush breasts to him. She was in as bad of shape as he was; the need was a living, breathing thing. There would not be any interruptions, not tonight. Not for the next several days, years, centuries — whatever it took to make her his.

CHAPTER NINETEEN

The trip down the stairs was the longest Aaron had ever taken. Of course, if they hadn't stopped several times, pressing against the wall for support, kissing and touching, it may have been a little faster, but their need was out of control.

Aaron barely got her into the room, slamming the door shut with his foot before they were kissing and making their way to his bed.

"Baby, we need to slow down. We have the rest of our lives for this. I want you to enjoy this."

"Then, Aaron, if you want us to live that long, long enough for us to live together, I suggest you get out of your clothes and take me."

Aaron reached down and cupped her ass in his hands, marveling at the way she fit against him. He lifted her then, pulling her body up against his, her sex meeting up with his hard length. She moaned, he growled, both needing more than the contact they were getting while fully dressed.

"I want you, Sara." He growled. His voice was hard and heavy with his desire.

"Yes. Oh, yes, please," she growled back.

He smiled; she wasn't in any better shape than he was, apparently. Aaron set her down on her feet, never breaking contact with her mouth. He began to unbutton the buttons down the front of her shirt, finally pulling it apart with a sharp tug, buttons flying every which way. With her torso exposed, he reached down and pulled his own shirt over his head. He could feel Sara's hot breath on his skin; he wanted to touch her to him, bring her body as close to his as a couple could get. Then he was looking down at the tiny scrap of lace holding her breasts from him. He began to work at the closure on the front with slow progress. He moved his hands against her breasts with the barest of touches, brushing against them. When he finally unhooked it, her breasts spilled out into his hands.

Mine.

Aaron pulled away from her mouth to look down at the treasure he had just exposed. Reaching out, Aaron gently cupped each plump mound in his hands, lifting them up to feel the weight. Her nipples, a dusty rose color, were puckered tight against the creamy flesh of her breasts. He ran his thumb over each nub and watched as Sara's head fell back as if to surrender to him. Leaning down, he took the first nipple into his mouth, laving it with his tongue and then sucking it hard into his mouth. He reached over to her other breast and began to pull, rolling the nipple hard between his thumb and finger, feeling it tighten in his hand. Not to leave the other breast out, he changed positions and suckled the other deeply, rolling it with his talented tongue against the roof of his mouth. He wanted to be gentle, but her moans were making him hurt with need, and all he could think about was being inside of her.

Aaron took her open palm and ran it down his chest, over his own nipples, now as hard as hers. He continued down, guiding her slowly. He watched her face, watched as she discovered him, his furred chest, and muscles of his belly. Down he took her, down to his belt and lower. When he stroked his cock with her hand, she closed her eyes and moaned.

"No, Sara, not yet. I want to watch you. I want you to see how you make me feel when you touch me."

Sara opened her eyes. This time, he moaned. She was magnificent.

"I love touching you, feeling your length in my hand. Aaron, please. Please, I ache so badly."

Aaron pulled her up high on his body so he could continue his torment on her breasts, walking her backward toward his bed. When his knees bumped the mattress, he stopped, sliding her down his body, wrapping her around him. He worked the button and zipper open on her pants and slid his hands behind her and into them. Hot, bared skin filled his hands. With her arms around his neck and her legs locked around him, he laid her onto the bed beneath him, cupping and massaging her ass the whole time. Breaking the kiss, he unhooked her lovely legs from his waist and moved down her body to undress her completely. With her feet hanging off the end of the bed and him on his knees between them, he pulled her hips up, and the jeans and panties came off together. They were tossed to the floor, and he looked at the beauty before him.

Sara's curls between her thighs were wet with need. Aaron ran his hands along her knees and up to her thighs. He looked up at her just as she sat up and leaned on her elbows.

"Sara, love, are you sure?" He'd die if she said no now. He'd stop, but he'd be dead all the same.

"Your eyes....they're red and bright. Is it because of me, because of what we're doing?"

"Yes. My need for you, my hunger to claim you, to be inside you, is bringing out the beast in me." He started to step back from her, but she stopped him with her feet at his hips. "Are you afraid?"

Long seconds passed before she answered. "No. I'm not afraid of you. I know you won't hurt me."

"No, I won't hurt you. I can't hurt you. You're my mate, Sara. I've searched for you for centuries. I'd nearly given up on finding you." He touched her now, gently, reverently.

"No. I...Aaron, you should know...." She looked away from him, and he stopped touching her, suddenly afraid.

"What is it, love?"

"I've never done this before. I don't know what to do to please you. I feel…I think you should also know that I love you. I feel as if I've waited my whole life for you as well."

"Oh, Sara, I love you so much. You already have pleased me, more than you know. And I have waited for you, Sara, for over a thousand years. I want you very much. But if you want to stop, we will."

Again, she stared up at him; he could feel her in his mind, searching for the truth of his words.

"You would, wouldn't you? Stop, I mean?" she asked him, surprise evident in her voice.

"Yes. Now I can, but later, I don't know if I'll be able to." He grinned at her. He knew that if she stopped him at any point, he would, just as she knew he would too.

Aaron ran his hand further up her leg, just at the juncture of her thighs. He ran his finger along her nether lips, never taking his eyes from hers. Slowly, he entered her with his finger, and then just as slowly, pulled out again. He did this several times, in and out, in and out. He added another, stretching her body, readying it for his cock. Her hips began to undulate around his finger; she began to move hard against him. Her cream began to soak his fingers, then his hand.

"I want you, Sara; I want to be doing this with my cock. I want to fuck you. I need to fuck you." He moved faster, deeper inside of her, her heat, her wetness making it easier and easier for him to slide inside of her.

"Yes," she said with a hiss of need.

Sara's head was thrown back now, her body moving against his fingers in a seductive imitation of sex. His cock was hurting against his zipper; he needed to relieve the pressure before he hurt himself. As it was now, he was sure he had an imprint of the zipper teeth tattooed on his skin. With his other hand, he rubbed it along his cock. He knew he wouldn't last long, but he needed her to have as much pleasure as he could give her this first time.

Aaron leaned forward and slid his tongue inside of her, teasing her clit, tasting her cream, the unique taste that was hers and hers alone. Her body stiffened, bowed up off his bed, and then suddenly, she came apart with a scream. Her climax roared through him, over him. He let her ride him, his tongue lapping up every drop of her climax, her juices flowing from her, soaking his hand, coating his face. When she lay lax beneath his mouth, he pulled his fingers free. He had to fight the urge to continue tasting her, even for the few minutes it took to reach down and unsnap and pull the zipper tab down. His cock sprang free from its confines. The need to be inside of her overwhelming. He wasn't sure if he could be gentle any longer. He stood up and quickly undressed himself the rest of the way until he stood before her, nude. His cock was hard, harder than it had ever been. She looked up at him and licked her lips. He fisted his cock and stroked it up and down, watching her face, seeing her need was as sharp as his own. He thought to come like this, masturbating while she watched just to take the edge off. He knew she would enjoy it, as she had before. This time, he would be able to come all over her nakedness, over her breasts.

"Sara, baby, I need you. But I don't want to hurt you. Help me come, touch me like before. I need to come on you, honey."

She reached for him, pulling him closer to the edge of the bed. When she wrapped her small hand around him, he jerked hard. Christ, she was hot. As his knees wobbled a bit, he leaned hard into her hand. His weight toppled him on top of her and onto the bed.

"Baby, I'm sorry, I can't wait any longer. I need to fill you; I need to be inside of you."

"Thank goodness! Please hurry, Aaron. Hurry before I have to hurt you."

As a sudden chuckle left his mouth, he moved up her body, tasting as he went, nipping at her flesh here and there, driving her need higher with each touch of his mouth. Her body was taut. He could tell she was close, and this time, when she came, he was going to be deep inside of her.

"Please, Aaron, now, please. I want you, I want you now."

"Baby, please don't move. I'm barely hanging on here. Give me a minute." His cock was at the mouth of her core. He could feel her heat pulling at him. He knew that he needed to go carefully into her, or he would surely hurt her.

"Aaron, if you don't move inside of me, I may stake you yet, I swear it."

Aaron laughed. "This is not a time to be cracking jokes, love. I don't want to hurt you, but all I can think about is slamming my cock hard into you, taking you and making you mine."

But he found that she had unknowingly taken an edge off of his primal need to claim. He felt himself ease and knew that now he wouldn't hurt her. She moved against him again. He moaned long and hard.

The next time she moved, he thrust forward into her, breaking through her maidenhead. He took several deep breaths before he spoke, leaning his forehead against hers, his need to move inside her making him sweat.

"Sara, are you all right? I'm sorry, there was no other way, but it won't hurt again, I swear. If you want to stop, we will, just as soon as I can move. Sara, answer me. Are you okay?"

He looked down at her; he could see the wetness in her eyes, but no tears on her cheeks.

"Hi." He smiled down at her.

"Hello. You're inside me," she whispered to him.

"Yes, just about. Do you hurt? Did I hurt you much?" He moved his hips just a little as he whispered back to her and nearly wept with relief when she moved back against him.

"Just about? What do you mean, there's more of you? A lot more?" She moved beneath him, and he rocked forward another inch.

They both moaned at the feeling. Her body was rapidly adjusting to his size and length. Her heat was scorching him, her body pulling him in further, milking and squeezing him.

"Yeah, but only about another six or seven inches." At the look on her face, he laughed again. Who would have thought that at a time like this, they could be laughing? "No, I'm only kidding." And with that, he pushed forward the last two inches, seating himself fully inside her, touching her womb.

Aaron looked at her face then and thought he had never seen anything so beautiful in his long life. He moved his hips, bringing himself nearly out, then slowly moved back inside of her. It didn't take him long to find a rhythm, taking this first time as slowly as he could, getting her used to him and what they were doing. Sara apparently had other ideas.

She surged up against him harder with each of his downward thrusts. Behind him, she hooked her ankles at his hips. He could feel her need for more clawing at him. His need for more grew stronger with each stroke of his cock, every time she gripped her nails into his shoulders and back.

"Sara! Christ, woman, you feel so good, so tight." Aaron could feel his own climax climbing up his back, moving around to his cock, and his balls tightened against him. He was ready to explode. He didn't think he was going to be able to hold out much longer. He reached between them and palmed her breast, pulling and tugging on her nipple, her own moans of pleasure driving him mad.

Aaron's need to complete the bond between them overwhelming; he wanted…no, he needed…to sink his teeth into her, taste her essences, and fill his body with her. He kissed her jaw, making his way toward the long line of her throat. He could feel his fangs bursting from his gums, and he was almost to the point of pain. The need was so incredible. He licked the pulse, beating there as hard as his. He had to have her.

"Sara…I want to taste you, sip from you. I need you, baby."

He pulled the rapidly beating pulse in his mouth and suckled it hard.

"Aaron, oh God, please, bite me. Bite me now!"

He sank his fangs into her jugular deep; her essences burst into his mouth. *Mine,* his heart claimed, *all mine.* He drew in another mouthful. He jerked his mouth away when the tide of the climax seized him. He roared her name as he came, pouring inside her, spurting and spurting into her, touching her womb with every stroke.

Aaron had never come so hard or for so long in all his life. He could still feel her body pulling and milking him, still in the aftermath of her own climax. He dropped his full weight onto her small frame, rolled to his side, taking her with him so that she was across him rather than under him. When he felt her warm blood on his chest, he realized he hadn't sealed the bite and pulled her to him to do so.

"Sara, are you all right?" He sealed the tiny wounds with his tongue. Already, he could feel his need for her building again. His cock, still hard inside of her, twitched with renewed energy. When she rocked against him, his breath caught.

"I don't know if I can talk yet. Give me, oh I don't know, a couple of years, then I can have a conversation with you. Right now, I want to...."

Aaron pulled her face up to look at her, to see if she was hiding something from him, pain she wasn't telling him about. "You want to what, love?"

"Did you...hmmm...did you enjoying being with me? I know you...you know, but did you enjoy it? I gotta tell you, that was the biggest rush I've had since I learned how to tuck and roll in a plane!"

Aaron burst out laughing. Only Sara, he thought, his Sara. He wanted to be insulted but just couldn't. She was delightful and happy. What man wouldn't want to be compared to a trick in an airplane and have a naked, sexy woman on top of him doing it?

Aaron shifted her suddenly so that she was across him fully. His blood turned molten. He was becoming richer, stronger because of her. She pulled her mouth away from his, sat up, and rode him, pulling him deeper inside her. He took her hands and put them to her breasts, showing her what he wanted her to do, sending her pictures of what he needed.

Sara looked down at him. His eyes were glowing red; his need was so high, so deep, she began to pull and tug on her nipples, filling her hands with their weight. He dug his hands painfully into her hips, slamming her hard against his cock, driving her deeper onto him.

"Sara, I'm coming!" He flipped her over onto her back, bit into her neck, and rammed his cock into her harder, deeper than he had before. This time, when he came, she was there with him, coming and coming over and over with each thrust of his cock, each pull of his mouth.

Finally, when he could move again, he rolled over and pulled her over him. She never stirred, never woke up, and he slept as well.

CHAPTER TWENTY

Later, when they woke up, Aaron stiffened when he heard Sara moan quietly. He knew she'd be weak and sore, hurting from their lovemaking and her giving him blood. Aaron decided that a nice soak in the big tub in the large bathroom would alleviate some of the soreness. When the tub was full of hot water, he picked her up from the bed and carried her like the precious cargo she was into the room. He wouldn't even let her stand. He could see she was indeed worn out and stepped into the tub with her still in his arms. As he slowly sank them both beneath the warm water, he positioned her in front of him between his legs with her back to his chest so that he could anchor her to him, to hold her above the water.

The bathroom here in his lair seldom got used, with the exception of the shower. It was as big as some people's apartments. The walls were all imported handmade tile of the richest blues and reds. They not only covered the floor but three of the walls as well. The forth wall, the one just over the nine-by-nine foot garden tub, was a bank of quarried stone. The double sink and separate shower and tub fixtures were made of gold and shone brightly in the room. The other fixtures, such as the toilet and countertop, were a deep shade of red. The sink basins were large, deep pottery bowls of cobalt blue. The only other colors in the room were the towels hanging on the warmer and were of the purest white.

Aaron sprayed water over her head, careful not to get soap in her eyes, and gently began to wash and rinse her hair. Then using a large bath sponge, he washed her body of the sweat from their lovemaking.

Neither said anything for a long time. They just enjoyed holding and touching each other, not always in a sexual, sensual way, just the need to connect on some level, to be together at last. The candles that Sara had lit twinkled gently around the room; their jasmine scent delicately moved throughout the room.

"I wondered if my abilities would change if you bit me. I don't think they did, but they're different, stronger in some ways, sharper in others. I can also feel a deeper connection to you. I can hear your heart beating, mine too." She turned around on his lap and looked at him. "I can also feel Sherman; his presence is there, just in the back of my mind. I could feel him before, but not like this. Before, I was aware of him because I was worried about Mel. Now, he's just there. I feel his hatred more."

"What about the others? Can you feel them as well?" He thought about Sherman, wondering about what he was going to do about him.

He felt her stiffen slightly. "Demetrius and April are making love. Again. Sheesh, is that all they can think about?"

"Again? You know what, never mind. I don't want to know. Moving along, unless you want to let me watch and take notes. And I'd like to point out, you and I have made love several times just tonight."

"You do just fine on your own." She snuggled back against him. "I am hungry, really hungry, as a matter of fact. Do you think Duncan has anything in the house?"

"I don't know. We could order something or go out if you'd like." He hadn't thought of human food for a long while. He'd had Duncan get some into the house for her when she was staying there before, but that couldn't be any good now. The thought of her eating something was making him hard again, and he didn't even know why.

"No, I want a cheeseburger with lettuce and tomato. Pickles, lots of pickles. And so much catsup and mayo that it drips down my hands. Hmmm. I wanna bite down into a really fresh bun. Oh, and french fries. Gotta have fries with a cheeseburger. You have to soak up the drippy stuff off the plate with them. I like to eat them two or three at a time. I love them overcooked and salty, really...Aaron, I'm really hungry."

Aaron stared at her for all of twenty seconds and then stood the both of them up in the tub, splashing water all over the bathroom floor. He wanted to see her eat real food. He'd never had a cheeseburger himself; they weren't around when he was human, but he could watch people eat them. And he was very excited about seeing her eating one, sinking her teeth into one, chewing it, savoring it just like she had described. Christ, he had a hard-on thinking about her eating food. He was in serious trouble here.

Aaron dressed with the speed only vampires have, blurring through the room, finding her something of his to wear. They were upstairs and in the kitchen in record time and going through the refrigerator searching for ground beef, lettuce, tomatoes, and pickles, everything that went on a burger with the works. They didn't have any luck with the french fries, but they made do with a bag of green onion chips in the cabinet.

Sara made the patty and put it into the large skillet they'd unearthed under the counter. The smell of sizzling beef permeated the room. While that cooked, she sliced the tomatoes and pickles. He was mesmerized as she put one in her mouth and sucked it. He was sure she wasn't even aware of what she was doing to him. Then again, maybe she was.

By the time she ate a cheeseburger with all the trimmings and was dipping up a big bowl of ice cream, he was hard as stone. When she searched for something to top the last bit of creamy confection, she came across a can of whipped cream. Aaron's eyes were on her ass as she was bent over looking, and when she stood and turned toward him, his eyes had turned with need.

Aaron stood up from the chair, undoing the snap and zipper on his low rider jeans as he approached her. When his cock was free, he stopped in front of her and began stroking it with his fist, up and down, up and down. She watched him, mesmerized by his hand, fisting his cock. By the time the drop of pre-cum pearled at the tip, he could smell her arousal on his tongue.

"Suck my cock. Suck me until I come in your mouth. I want to shoot my hot cum down your throat." She dropped to her knees without a second's hesitation, licking her lips. Her tongue darted out and captured the drop at the tiny slit at the head of his cock. She climaxed as soon as she tasted him. Aaron leaned forward to hold onto the counter, his release ready to explode from him as he watched her come.

"Sara, please, now, take me now." Before the last word spilled from his mouth, she wrapped her mouth around him.

Her mouth was hot and wet, tight like her. He couldn't hold back. He reached down and cupped the back of her head. Holding her head gently, he began pumping his length in her, fucking her mouth like he had her body. He wanted to be easier, not rock so hard, but when she wrapped her hand around his length, he started pumping like a man possessed. He looked down at her through hooded eyes and saw her riding her own fingers, riding them like he was fucking her like he was fucking her mouth. His climax grabbed him, he roared as he released deep into her mouth, and she swallowed every drop. When the last of his cum spurted into her luscious mouth, he jerked her up and slammed her onto the counter, tearing away the shirt and panties. He rammed his still hard cock deep inside her, fast. It didn't take long for him to come again, and as soon as he bit her, she came with him, screaming and sobbing his name over and over again.

~~~

Aaron watched her sleep. It wasn't the deep sleep of his kind, but of the exhausted sleep of a woman well used throughout the night. He smiled down at her. She was his mate.

Sara would never be boring, that was for sure. He was looking forward to many, many years with her beside him and him beside her. He kissed her gently on her brow, careful not to disturb her. They had made love, sometimes bordering on violent at times, several times tonight. She needed to rest, and he needed to go and find Colin.

They needed to set in motion better security for his home. He also wanted Colin to search for as much information as he could about Shermie, Mel's mate, and what he'd been up to since Mel had gone into hiding. He also wanted to know if he'd been the one beating Sara all this time. If he had, then there wasn't going to be a realm, human or magical, that he could hide in that Aaron wouldn't be able to find him.

Aaron was back long before daybreak, finding he couldn't be without her. He was drifting off to slumber, smiling and thinking about what a turn on it had been to watch her eat a burger. He couldn't wait to tell Duncan to get a good supply of burger fixings and fries in the house. Duncan was going to be pissed about the mess in the kitchen, or maybe not. Duncan had become very lax about things when it came to Sara. Sex, at least like they had had on a counter, was not very neat and tidy.

CHAPTER TWENTY-ONE

That evening when Aaron rose, Sara was gone. He was up and getting dressed to find her when she whispered through his mind.

"Good morning. Did you sleep well, bloodsucker?" He felt her laughter race across his skin like a touch.

"Good morning yourself, human. Yes, I slept very well. Someone wore me out completely. Where are you, love? I thought you'd be here when I arose."

"I have a job. Some of us aren't wealthy and can't laze about all day in bed." He felt her laughter again, her voice doing all sorts of things to his libido.

"I thought we'd spend the day in my bed, getting to know each other...better." He sent her waves of his need for her. He felt when she became so aroused that it was uncomfortable for her. That made him smile.

"Stop that," she told him breathlessly. *"I'm at about twenty-five thousand feet right now, so I don't need to get all hot and bothered by you just yet. I can come over after I land. Would that be okay?"*

"I want you here all the time, Sara. Move in here with me, stay with me?" He knew that this should have been something he asked her in person, but his heart and his body couldn't wait.

"We'll talk when I come over. I…I'm not...I don't...."

"It's all right, love." And he realized that it was. He loved her. *"When you come over, we'll talk, okay? I don't want to force you into anything you don't want. I just need to see you."*

"Okay then. I will land in about forty-seven minutes, and then it will take me about twenty-three minutes to get to your house. I'll see you then?" He heard the relief in her voice and tried not to be hurt by it.

Only Sara would give exact times. He grinned. He knew that she was correct in the amount of time it would take her to land and be at his house. Why? Because she was Sara.

"All right, I'll see you then. Oh and Sara, don't eat anything. I had Duncan get you some stuff to eat. I want to see you eat those french fries."

~~~

Sara landed the beautiful Cessna just over forty-eight minutes later, taxiing to the hangar on a perfect landing. She was reaching out to Aaron to let him know she was running behind when she felt them in the hangar. The High Council had finally come for her. She got off the plane and went straight to them. She felt there was no reason to run. They'd find her again anyway.

"Sara, please don't fight us," Tyler Sims, second in command of the Royal Guard, pleaded with her. "You know that in this world, we'd have to kill you immediately if you do."

Sara looked at the men before her and sighed. She could easily kill them all, even without her armament. They were an untried and young group of men and women. Marcus had told her that most of the others, the more seasoned and trained, had fled, taking their families away when Sherman had taken over Molavonta after Mel had disappeared. Most, if not all of them, were hiding in the human realm until things returned to normal. She wondered if that would ever be possible now.

"I won't fight," she told him as she put her arms forward, palms out. No, she wouldn't fight them. She needed to let Aaron know what had happened and to contact Mel to take care of their bond. She wouldn't have him die because of her.

Two men stepped forward and clamped the leg shackles and wrist irons on her. Drawing his sword, Tyler walked toward her.

She could tell that he was scared and nervous.

"I won't fight you, Tyler, I promise you."

At his nod, he touched it to the skin just over her heart. As soon as he touched her skin with his sword, they were in Molavonta standing outside one of the dungeons' doors.

"I'm sorry, Sara," he told her as soon as the others left them alone. "But I thought if I was with you, you'd stand a better chance of getting here in one piece. Orders were to kill on sight if you put up the least resistance."

"I figured as much. When...do they have a time set yet?" She couldn't ask when her beheading was. It was too much. Her heart crumbled in pain. Aaron, oh, Aaron.

"There's to be a trial first. I've never heard why. Usually, they just take the accused out and lop off their.... Oh my God, Sara, I'm sorry. I...I wasn't thinking," Tyler said.

"It's all right, really. If you could, could you maybe keep me informed? Not at risk to yourself, but you know...?" She couldn't look at his stricken face any longer and turned toward the cell door. As she slid inside, he moved beside her.

"This is from the queen," he whispered as he put a small stone in her hand and slipped back out again. In a louder voice, he said, "Yes, when I know, you'll know."

~~~

When April and Demetrius came into their office at the airstrip, Melody was answering the company phones. It would have been comical if they hadn't heard what she was saying.

"Yes, I'm pretty sure we fly there, too. No, no, I don't know anything about planes, big or little. Other than they can fly, of course. When I want to be somewhere, I just zap myself there.... No, I don't want to zap you anywhere, but if you keep being stupid, I might just zap you." She turned to them as she was hanging up the now dead receiver. "He hung up on me, the nerve. Hi, we have a problem."

Demetrius knew that if Melody the Queen was here, then

something had seriously gone wrong. He'd just leave this time, not stand and fight. He couldn't chance losing April and the child. He looked around the beautifully appointed office. All the leather on the chairs and chrome tables were more to his tastes rather than April's, but she had been getting used to it. He loved the shelves, though. They held some of the most unique model planes he'd ever done. He'd carved them all by hand over the centuries.

The photos on the wall were of birds and kites and other flights of fancy, all precursors to the flight of man. The windows looked out over the large, wooded area on the back lot, where they were currently having their home built. This room's dark paneling made it seem homey and warm despite the modern touches. All the clean lines and smell were usually relaxing, but it wasn't working right now — too much stress in his personal life with the new baby and poor Sara.

"Yes, we do, if you have been here all day answering the phone. Why the hell are you here?" April asked.

Demetrius could feel the anger boil off both women. April had taken exception to the woman since the party. Just last night, she had been telling him how much she hated the way she'd treated Sara after all she'd done for her. He secretly agreed. Sparks were going to fly between the two women. He just hoped it was later rather than today.

"You know I can read your every thought," said the queen.

Demetrius flushed. He'd forgotten that about her.

After a few tense moments of the two women staring at each other, Mel turned to Demetrius again. "Sara's been arrested by the High Council. They came here and picked her up about an hour ago. I can only assume they knew to come then because you two would be out. She's being detained in one of the cells in the dungeon. And before you ask, yes, she's being treated very well. For as much as you'd like to believe I'm a horrible ruler, I do have people in place I can trust."

"Then you can have her released, right?" It seemed simple enough to Demetrius. Just pop in say, "release her," and she'd be home again.

"No. Right now, that's not possible," Mel told them.

"Then what the hell good are you? Let me ask you something, do you think that if you were in trouble, she'd not break down every door in that place to get to you in a heartbeat? That she wouldn't go against everything she stands for to save your skinny little ass? Hell, she did do that at great risk to herself. And this is the way you repay her? By sitting on your ass, acting all queenie like?" Demetrius reached out to pull April back before she did something stupid. She simply brushed him off.

"Why you bloodsucking, stupid...." Mel snarled at his mate as she stood to advance on April.

"That's enough! Christ, you two can take this up later. How do you propose we help her if you can't help us? Because I, for one, would lay down my life for her." She had risked her life, damn it! For him, for April, and especially for his babe. He'd stay. For her, he'd stay.

"As I said...." With a glare at April, Mel continued. "She can't be released just yet. It's important that, at least for a while longer, everyone believes that she did something to me."

April's mouth opened in shock. "So, let me get this straight; we wait until someone notices that you're okay before we go in and get her? You know, as far as planning well goes, you really suck at it." April wanted to hit the woman. Demetrius could tell by the way she kept flexing her fist.

"April, this isn't getting us any closer to Sara and getting her free. You can kill the queen later...provided we have the time, that is." He sat down heavily in the office chair. "Is Sara hurt?"

"No. I told you, she's being well taken care of. I have a trusted guard outside her cell at all times. No one will get in there without a fight." At Demetrius's nod, she went on. "Aaron. Someone needs to go and explain what's happened to her."

"And tell him what? You haven't told us a damned thing. All you've told us is that Sara's been arrested on trumped-up charges because you aren't dead. Yet. And we can't tell anyone you're alive. Gee, that'll go over well, don't you think?" April snarled.

"You know you're very sarcastic. I know you're trying to hide it and all, but you're doing a piss poor job of it. Maybe you should practice a bit more. You're just not quite perfect at it yet. I can still hear when you're being sincere," Mel said. Even Demetrius could hear the venom in her voice. "He'll need to be told everything I've told you. Aaron needs to let this progress to the trial. If he interrupts, lives could be at stake."

"What do you mean, lives? Sara's? Oh no, you don't, you'll explain better than that. I've had enough of your partial information." April advanced on her and would have gone further if Demetrius hadn't stopped her by pulling her into his lap and holding her down.

"Sherman is strong, very strong, and I believe he wants to kill Sara for her powers. If he does, he will be unstoppable," Mel said.

"Why would he have to kill her for her powers? Why can't he just fade her or whatever, like he did to you?" Demetrius knew what Sherman had done to Mel when Sara had had to save her. He also knew the extent of the damage he'd done to her mentally as well as physically. Causing her to miscarry the only child she would ever have, being the worst of the damage as far as Demetrius was concerned. He didn't know what he would do if April lost their child. He couldn't imagine being the cause of her losing it.

"I don't know what Sara is," Mel admitted sadly. "If she isn't a royal like I'm assuming Sherman believes her not to be, then he will need only to kill her. He will then be able to absorb her powers into himself, making him incredibly strong. As far as I can tell, that would make him nearly impossible to destroy as a true immortal. He's been practicing black arts or magic. While I do have control over all magic, black is the most unstable. White or pure magic, which most witches practice, is a give and take system. Earth gives you its powers to use."

Demetrius watched as things began to appear around Mel as she walked. A basket of fruit filled with apples, pears, and bananas, a glass of wine. She took each thing and sampled it as she continued to pace the small room. She seemly didn't even realize what was happening.

"Once you use what you need, you give back to her ten times that amount. Its recycled energy is used in the colors of flowers: yellows, pinks and reds, also in the green of the tree leaves. There are also creatures that can change the colors, but the magic must be there, the magic of the earth, to sustain their magic. The purer the magic returned, the brighter the colors in the fauna in that area.

"Black magic is not renewable. It only takes from the earth, and most importantly, from the user. It also burns them up very fast. That's the reason people who practice it are always in packs. They nearly always have to combine their resources to make whatever magic they're using last for longer than a few minutes. Once someone in the pack begins to grow in power, he's killed." A flurry of her hands and a hologram of a field appeared, and on it, several figures. Suddenly, one broke free and killed one of the others. A patch of blackened earth appeared in his place, then the entire scene disappeared. "They'd rather kill than have one of their kind get strong enough to overpower them," Mel explained.

"And if she is a royal? What then? Will she be able to destroy him? I thought that as a royal, he would be an immortal like you. I guess I don't understand the differences between an immortal or a royal," Demetrius said.

"I'm a true immortal because of my birth. I cannot die." He watched as Mel reached over and touched the violet on the desk. It suddenly doubled in size and overflowed with fat purple blossoms. "I can fade away if I choose, but that isn't death. It's not permanent."

She sat in the chair again, looking exhausted and worn. "I've just called my mother home from Ireland where she's been a fairy ring for centuries. Sherman isn't a royal by blood, just by mating with me. When we claimed each other so that he could be with me forever, he became a true immortal by proxy. That's the only way we could spend eternity together. And so long as I don't denounce him publicly, he'll continue to be. The only way to destroy or kill him he must do one of three things; he must kill another royal, attempt the life of an immortal, or be stripped of his status. Any one of the first two will automatically strip him down to his former self, but then he will still have his magic and will need to be killed."

"So, his attempt on your life should have taken away his immortality. But it didn't, why?" April asked her with no hostility in her voice at all, Demetrius was relieved to realize.

"Not unless someone in the High Council is aware of his involvement in the plot. I doubt that, when Sara was fleeing the castle with my body after the explosion, she hung around to explain what happened. And without my body...." Mel shrugged. "I'm sorry to say that she was guilty until proven innocent. No, Sherman is more than likely sanctioned by the Council because they believe that Sara and the others failed me or were the ones who committed the crime. It is in all likelihood that Sara is a wanted fugitive."

"Then he's the one who had her arrested." At her nod, he continued. "High Council of Magick? You've mentioned that before. Is that some sort of court system or something?" Demetrius asked her, trying hard to understand a whole other world other than the two he currently lived in.

"Yes, that's exactly what they are. I am magic, but without someone to govern even me, things could be one sided. The Council wants for nothing. The people see to their needs. So they enforce my law for me. If not for someone to back me up and with nothing to gain, I could become a tyrant." She looked at April. So did he. But his mate just smiled at them both and continued as if Mel hadn't given her a perfect shot.

"That probably explains why she is working for smaller airlines, and when she does fly for the bigger companies, she does it under the company name and not her own. She is hiding out, just not from anyone in the human world. All this time, we believed her to be hiding from the law. Just never imagined that it was the law of another realm," Demetrius mused out loud.

"What happens if she is able to prove Sherman is the one who caused your demise? Is he then stripped of his royal sanction?" April asked her.

"Yes, and once that happens, he'll be a mere immortal. Then... then Sara will be able to fry his ass," she stated with a huge smile.

CHAPTER TWENTY-TWO

Sara waited until full darkness before she opened her hand to the bright orange stone. Looking toward the door to make sure no one could see her, she blew gently across it.

She'd been given one of these stones before, a blue one then. It had been many years ago when she was still being tested and trialed to become a guard. The instructions had been to open it. It had taken her several hours of studying it, rubbing it between her hands, throwing it. She'd even tried soaking it in water. As she was drying it off, she blew a piece of lint off it, and it opened up, revealing the message.

The stone rocked softly in her hand, vibrating little shakes. As she watched, the stone began to morph; tiny wings began to separate themselves from its surface. Then a face formed and took shape, its features so small they looked surreal.

As the wings started to flutter, the rest of the stone became arms, legs, and a body. The little creature rolled over in Sara's palm and stretched tautly. It was a pixie, a woodland being that worked with the forest. Sara watched as the pixie pulled her little wings tightly against her back as she continued to change and become whole.

When it had rested for several minutes, it suddenly flew from her hand and across the room toward the sink. Then she flitted over to the toilet and around the rim. Her wings were going so fast that it was nearly impossible to see with the human eye. Sara watched her until she came back and landed on her bent knee.

Sara smiled at her. She wasn't at all what the movies portrayed a pixie to look like. Her wings were diaphanous, of course. But the rest of her was purely female. Her short hair was bright, bright orange and spiked all over her head. Her eyes were also orange, but not quite as bright as the hair. She had a piercing in her little nose and a chain of something sparkly around her ankle. In addition to the dark green Grateful Dead t-shirt, she also had on a pair of Capris that reached just below her knees and flip-flops.

"Don't you just hate Ohio weather? It can be hotter than the Sarnillian's belly one day and colder than Daphne's tit the next." Her voice was tiny and squeaky, but Sara could hear her.

"I'll have to take your word for those places. You have a name, pix?" Sara asked her.

"Yeah, well, duh. Everyone has one, don't they? Sheesh, the queen said you were smart. It's Mari. Well, it's really Marigold, but I go by Mari. Do you believe this flippin' hair? I wanted to be pink, but that girl Petunia beat me to it." Mari began flipping her hair around with her fingertips.

"You mean there can only be one pink...you know, I don't care. You have a message for me, Mari?" Sara hated dealing with pixies. They tended to be self-centered and not a little narcissistic. This one was proving to be both.

"Yeah, the queen said to sit tight and not to do anything stupid. I guess we can mark that one off the list. You are in a dungeon. I'm also supposed to tell you that your vamp is well. You know a vampire? Oooooohhhh, has he nipped you yet? I would love to be bitten by one. That would be so cool," Mari gushed.

"He'd crunch you in half. What does she mean, sit tight?" Sara's head was beginning to ache already, and the pix had only been there five minutes.

"I don't know, just sit tight. You know that really is a stupid statement. Are you supposed to pucker up your butt while you sit here? Stupid. And I bet if you asked nicely, he'd bite me. Could you do that for me? I'd be your friend for life." Mari looked around the cell. "Okay, that really isn't a long time, but I could sneak you in some cigs to bribe the guards with."

"No, he's not going to bite you, and no, I don't want any cigarettes." Sara rubbed her forehead to try and ease some of the sudden tension. "As for the butt thing, I'm not even going to think about why you want to know. Can you take a message back to the queen for me?"

"Yeah, but you have to put me somewhere that I can get past the magick first. I can't break the ward put on the door to keep you in. Although why you'd want outta here is beyond me." Sara flicked her with her finger. Mari landed with a soft bump on the floor.

~~~

Aaron had been trying to contact Sara for nearly four hours when Demetrius shimmered into the room. He simply dropped to the nearest chair.

"What's happened? Did the plane go down? Please tell me she didn't suffer. Oh, Demetrius, I...."

"Sire, she's all right. I'm sorry, I never...I'm sorry, sire. She's... the queen, Melody, sent me to talk to you. She said that I needed to explain what's happened."

"Where is Sara? I need to see her. Where?" He reached for her again and was terrified once again at the finality of their connection. It was as if she no longer lived. "If she's all right like you say, why can't I reach her?" He stood up and began pacing.

"She's been arrested for—" Demetrius started

"Arrested! For what? She hasn't done anything wrong. Take me to her right now. We'll clear this up in no time." He began walking to the door. When he turned around, the other vamp was still sitting. "What else, Demetrius? What haven't you told me?" He sat down again. He suddenly felt his fourteen hundred years.

"Sara's been arrested for treason and murder. They have her in a dungeon in Malt...Mult...the castle. Melody said that you must not go to her, nor should you plan her escape. She also explained that you mustn't try and contact her, that Mel's mate must continue to think she, Mel, is gone."

CHAPTER TWENTY-THREE

Sara had been in the castle dungeon for three days with only a small patch of light from a vent high on the wall to mark her time. She wanted to see Aaron, just one more time before they passed judgment on her. She knew that she was to die, but they were slowly killing her by keeping her away from Aaron. She had stopped asking last night; no one paid any attention to her anyway. She was getting hoarse from screaming for someone to let her see him.

Sara's magic didn't work here; the cell was engineered in such a way to keep anyone inside from using anything to escape. Made sense if you thought about it, and she had. Every day, every hour, every second since she'd been tossed in here. She now sat in the corner of her cell, contemplating what had brought her to this end. Sherman. He seemed to be the bane of her misery.

Sara looked over at the tray of food from her evening meal. Her food was left untouched, as were the other meals that had been placed in the room. Her appetite was simply gone. It was too bad, really; it always looked like she was being fed more than bread and water. The bread that was there didn't look like it had one single worm in it either. She laughed manically at her own joke. They didn't serve food that way here. She knew that.

The cell really wasn't that bad either. There was a nice cot with a thick mattress on it. In addition to the clean sheets were two blankets and a fluffy pillow. It was by far softer than the back of her van had ever been. She'd fallen asleep in it twice, and while she didn't sleep well, it was no fault of the bed. There was a toilet and a sink with a plastic mirror over it. On the stone floor where she was currently sitting was a thick rug. There weren't any pictures on the walls, of course, but someone, long ago probably, had used something to carve his name in the dark stone. There were also a few crude words there, written well before Sara had been a thought in anyone's mind.

Sara felt them before she heard them unlocking the door. It was nearly time to come for the tray, so she didn't move when the door opened. That seemed to be the only power she had retained, feeling them but not reading their intent. So she was surprised when one of them touched her. He must have tried several times to speak to her, but she was too far gone in her depression to have heard him.

Sara looked up at him now, seeing him for the first time, and realized with a start it was Tyler. He looked so good to her. She nearly jumped up to hug him to her, so happy she was to see someone familiar. But her bonds, the shackles at her wrists and ankles, kept her from moving.

"Hello, Sara. Can you get up and follow me, please? The High Council is ready to see you now."

Sara looked at him for long moments and then turned back to the small patch of waning sunlight. "Lend me your dagger, Tyler, and leave me. Tell them you found me in my cell dead. I'd appreciate it. I don't want to die like a coward, and we both know the penalty for killing a royal blood." It was beheading at the gallows. They both had been witness to it enough. "I promise you it won't be a lie by the time you get back to them."

"Come on, up with you. You need to bathe and dress. The others are waiting to see you, and it isn't like you to keep people waiting. Come on." His voice held a bit of authority that she couldn't help but obey.

When she was standing, he let her go, and she crumbled to the floor again, bumping her head against the hard wall, not because she wouldn't go with him, but because she was weakened from lack of exercise and food.

"I'm so sorry. I've...I must have slipped." The sudden memory of saying that to someone nearly had her double over in pain. Oh, Aaron, she thought again.

"Steady there. No one will be happy if you are hurt," he told her as he held her tightly.

"Yes, can't have the condemned man, err, woman hurt before they behead her, can we?" She giggled manically again at her own joke. She was losing it, no doubt about it, she thought.

"See here now, girl, straighten yourself up. What's wrong with you? You're scaring the men. Steady yourself."

Tyler's tone and order had her trying to obey him before she could blink. Tricky bastard, he'd done that on purpose. She smiled slightly for the first time in days.

Tyler got her up, and though she was leaning heavily on him, they managed to traverse through the halls toward the lower bathhouse. He set her upon one of the chairs nearest the showers and hosed her down, clothes and all. She didn't think there would be any saving the shoes, but the chain maille's metal and arm and legs binds would be fine. They had taken her weaponry before putting her in the cell but had given her the dress of her position when she'd been a guard.

Tyler handed her a new bar of soap. She washed herself with no enthusiasm for the task. When he had hosed off the soapy film, she looked up at him and smiled.

"Thanks, Tyler. I do feel better. Where are you taking me? I suppose I should have inquired before, but I'm just...I guess it doesn't matter now, does it?"

"To the main Council Chamber. They're all gathered there." He had a squadron of twenty men with him, she noticed.

They must really be worried she'd freak out and start killing them all with this sort of manpower. A small laugh escaped her mouth before she could catch it. She was definitely going to need therapy after this. Then she thought, well, only if they have someone in the audience, come to think of it. Not much time for anything else.

"Are you hungry?" Tyler interrupted her musing. "They said that you haven't eaten much."

"No, I don't think so. My belly doesn't feel up to it. Maybe before they take me to the gallows, they could give me a cheeseburger and fries." Another memory and another sharp pain.

She burst into tears, and that quickly turned into heart-wrenching sobs. He held her until it passed, or at least slowed down enough so that they could be on their way.

One of the other guards brought in some clothes for her to wear, a pair of her jeans and a t-shirt. She put them to her nose and breathed deeply. He left her to her business, asking that she please let him know when she was dressed. In no time at all, she was opening the door and coming out.

"Come on then, let's get going," he told her. Her escort surrounded her completely, and off they went. She started whistling *Wizard of Oz* without thinking. One of the guards started to sing the words until Tyler cleared his throat. Spoilsport. Sara started humming the theme from *Jaws, Terminator,* then *Friday the Thirteenth* and any other horror movie she could think of as they made their way down the long corridors to her doom. By the time they rounded the last corner, she was singing "The End of the World As We Know It." However, she didn't feel fine.

~~~

Sara walked into the room with her head held high. Tyler had taken off her handcuffs so that she could bathe, but he hadn't replaced them, so she clasped her hands together before her. She didn't care. She wouldn't try to escape. She was tired of hiding, and she wouldn't endanger Aaron by letting him hide her in the human world, which she was sure he would be willing to do. No, this was much better; she could at least have her dignity this way.

Perhaps two hundred people were in the room, most of them standing behind the impromptu barrier that had been erected. Some were sitting in the stadium-like seating. Seven people were sitting behind a long table in the very back of the room, and another five sitting in chairs in front of it, facing her as well. This was where she was led to stand. She could feel the hostility and anger in the room. She didn't look to see why. Frankly, she was too depressed to care. She was above ground now, and her magic worked better. She simply didn't care enough to reach.

Sara looked back at the table and recognized a few of the faces staring back at her. One, in particular, was Robert Meal. He'd been the highest ranking officer of the High Council since she had started working for them. As the queen's personal guard, this council was the only one she and the other guard answered to aside from the queen and king of the realm. Also seated there was Sherman.

Shermie was sitting in one of the throne chairs. As this wasn't even close to the receiving room, or throne room, he must have had the chair brought in for him. *What a pompous ass*, she thought and gave him a small wave.

"Hello, Bob. How's it hanging? Shermie?" She laughed at him as he stiffened in pride. They'd always disliked her, and judging by the smirk, they were really enjoying this.

"Sara Temple, by order of the High Council and governing rulers of Molavonta, you've been brought before this council today to stand judgment for crimes against your queen. Do you know why?" Bob asked her with a grin. Yeah, she thought, he was really enjoying himself.

Before she could answer, there was a commotion behind her. As she turned fully to see what could have dared interrupt, she was engulfed in a pair of muscled arms and a very familiar scent. Aaron. Aaron held her close to him, kissing her face, ears, and neck, whatever he could touch. She, too, was holding onto him, clinging to him, knowing that any moment they would drag him away.

"Master Vampire MacManus, you will need to take your seat. These proceedings are underway, and you are not on trial here," Sherman said to him.

"No, I don't think so," Aaron said with defiance in his voice as he turned to the man. "I'm going to stand right here next to her. You can try and take me away, but I assure you, there are twice as many of us than there are of you. Blood will be shed if you try."

Aaron looked the man right in the eye, daring him to try. Sara knew that look. He'd used the same one on her numerous times over the past few weeks. She grinned. She didn't think poor old Shermie looked so happy now.

"This is not the way we do things, sir. I will ask you again to please be seated. If you do not comply, I will have the Royal Guard come in and take...."

Sara flexed her magic, just a small amount. The room seemed to swell then tighten. "He will stand with me."

Her voice was strong and held a great deal of authority. No one moved in the big room, nor did anyone speak for several long seconds. Shermie sat down.

"Very well then, Sara Temple, do you know why you are before this council?" His voice was a little wobbly at first but gained strength at the end. He apparently hadn't realized that she was this powerful. She hadn't moved at all.

"No."

"Do you have anything to say in your defense?" he asked without giving her any reason as to why she was there.

"I don't know what I'm defending myself against or for, so I can't say."

He ignored her, barely pausing before going onto his next question. "Is there anything you wish said on your own behalf?"

"Behalf of what? I don't have a clue of what I'm being held for." She was getting nervous. Someone was really pushing this thing through.

"Sara Temple, you leave me...I mean, you leave us no choice in this matter but to see that you are punished for the crime committed against the king. I, therefore —" He was cut off before he could continue with her supposed sentencing.

"My name is Thomas Shawn Reilly. I'm a vampire. My master is Master MacManus. I have something to say if you don't mind. I want to know what she is." Thomas stepped forward and bowed before Aaron, his master, and with a small nod from him, he turned to Sara and winked. "She heals like a supernatural, her speed is vampire fast, and you just experienced what I'm assuming is a small taste of her magic. I would like to know what she is before you destroy her because I have no doubt that's what you plan."

"Now see here." Sherman's eyes bulged in rage. "These hearings are conducted in a certain way. You people are not supposed to just...just...you need to sit down." All he needed to do now was stomp his foot, she thought, and he'd have a hissy fit down perfectly.

Another observer spoke up loud and clear. "I am Phillip, former guard to the queen and king to the first queen. I am magic. I think the doctor has a good point. I, too, would like to see what she is." He turned to Sara and asked, "Just how tight are you holding your shields, young lady?"

"I...I'm not sure what you mean." She looked around the room. She wouldn't run now, but out of habit, she looked for all the exits. She hated being the center of attention. Every instinct in her was flight or fight, and she was battling the flight part very hard.

"Yes, you do. Drop your shields, all of them. I want to feel your power run through you without them," Phillip told her gently.

"No," she insisted as she stepped back against Aaron. They didn't know what they were asking her to do.

"Sara, honey, do it for me, please?" Aaron pleaded with her as a whisper in her ear.

She looked at the man holding her. She understood what they were asking her to do. She just wasn't sure if it was such a good idea. But she couldn't refuse him. She would do anything for him. She reached out and hugged him to her, then stepped away. Her magic was very strong, even she knew that. When he reached toward her again, she shook her head at him and dropped her considerable hold on herself.

Every light bulb in the room brightened to the point of brilliance and then exploded. No one moved, and after a few seconds, the room lit up again with thousands of candlelights. Sara became luminescent in the darkened room. A pin dropping could have been heard, as everyone in the room had stilled. As her power moved throughout the room, it felt as if all of the air had been squeezed out of it. No one was unaffected by it. Then it eased as suddenly as it rose.

"I have only let it go all the way once before. Have you had enough yet?" She looked around the room at the people affected. Everyone seemed fine for now.

"No, let it go. You're still holding back, aren't you?" This was from one of the two men behind the table. Sara thought his name was James.

"Yes. I can't let it go with all these beings. It will hurt those that are sensitive if I release all of me. And anyone who isn't able to control their own powers, I can absorb theirs into me. The other...the person could die. I've learned to control it for reasons such as this. It's too strong for a room this small. You can't ask me to unleash myself around so many weaker beings."

"All right then, hold steady. Oh, by the way, I am James, mate and king to the second queen, and I, too, am magic. I want to gauge you and see if I can feel what you are."

Sara could feel him scanning her and started to tighten down again.

"No, don't do that. You're doing fine. I'm almost finished. You can't hurt me, love."

When James had finished, he sat down hard in his chair. He looked exhausted, spent. He leaned over to the woman sitting in the chair next to him. They whispered to each other for several minutes before she looked over at Sara. Then they resumed their conversation.

The woman stood up after twenty minutes had passed and walked over to where Sara and Aaron stood. There were tears in her eyes as Sara looked at her. Tears, she thought and looked closer at the woman. The tears triggered a long forgotten memory.

Sara was very small, and her mom had left her somewhere. As she frowned hard in concentration, Elizabeth reached up and smoothed the wrinkles.

"I am Elizabeth, First Queen to Magic and to Molavonta, the Keep in which we stand. I'm very glad to meet you, Sara Temple, Royal Guard." She turned back to the table and looked pointedly to Bob, then at Sherman. "And as such, I demand that these proceedings cease and desist immediately."

"Mistress," Bob cried. "This woman is brought before all here to be judged for murder and high treason. She murdered one of the Royal Guard. She has taken your own granddaughter and has done who knows what with her body. She must stand trial for these crimes." Bob's voice, while full of demands, was pleading as well.

Sherman shot up from his chair. "No. You will not rule here. I am king. She will stand trial for the fade of my mate. I will not tolerate her being free any longer. And poor David, his family is very dear to me. I must make her pay for his death as well."

"His name was Marcus, you simpleton," Elizabeth snapped at Sherman. "Dear friend indeed. You know, I believe it was you who threatened his family in the first place. Wasn't it you who told him that if he didn't comply, you'd kill him? Yes, it was him and the men you took into the human world to kill Master

Vampire MacManus. Why on earth should we...?"

Elizabeth paused when a swell of murmurs began at the back of the room and soon spread forward. As the crowd parted and bowed low, in walked Melody, dressed and crowned like the queen that she was. Out of habit and respect, Sara dropped to one knee, with bowed head, and saluted her as was her right as her queen. Leading her, dressed in his suit of armament, was Marcus, Master of the Royal Guard. And as Sara started to glance away, she caught sight of the pixie Mari perched on Mel's shoulder.

Elizabeth never turned around at any point of the noisy entrance Mel made. Sara watched from her position on the floor as Elizabeth offered her cheek to Mel. "About time," she grumbled to her.

"Are these the two people you were referring to? Seems to me this evidence alone should be enough to stop this stupidity err...I mean hearings. Again...what did you call him, love?"

Startled out of her amazement at seeing them all together, Sara answered. "Huhhhh, Shermie, mistress. I call him Shermie. He doesn't care for it, though."

"Well, that's what makes it fun, doesn't it?" she said with a wink. "Shermie, I'd like to have these proceedings stopped. Right now!"

~~~

Thomas looked from Sara to the man. "Well, what the hell is she?"

"Incredible! Yes, Sara is incredible," Phillip said for perhaps the eighth time. "And I've never come across anyone so strong. How on Earth have you stayed hidden for so long? No, don't answer that. You've been building up your shield to be as strong as your powers as they have increased, haven't you? Yes, that's the only way you could have stayed unfound like you have. Incredible!" James had been saying the same thing since they'd left the antechamber and adjourned back to the MacManus mansion.

"Phillip, dear," Elizabeth said, giving him a pointed look, "stop saying that. You're irritating me, and I have the patience of that very nice man Job. I can well imagine how you are affecting everyone else in the room."

She looked kindly toward Sara. "Child, we should have done this prior to invading you. I'm Elizabeth, as I've said. This is my mate, Phillip. The woman to my left is Savannah, and the man next to her is James. We're Melody's grandparents; Savannah and James are her parents. Melody asked us to come here to see if we could aid you in any way during those horrid trials. And I'm so glad she did. It is a pleasure to meet you."

"But we have met, haven't we? You are the woman from the shelter." The memory had clicked the moment she said she was Mel's grandparent.

"Yes. I wasn't sure you would have remembered. You were only a child at the time. Less than a year, I believe."

"Eleven months, I was eleven months old. My mother left me there. She said that she couldn't raise me without help, that my father was a no account liar, and I would be better off with the state."

"No, he wasn't," Elizabeth said as she sat down hard in one of the chairs. "Matthew was with me when she left you there. Matthew is…was…my son."

"Grandma, what do you mean 'your son?' I…isn't my mom your child? Matthew can't be your son. You're confused," Mel said to her grandmother. Sara burst out laughing at the look that passed between the two women. If looks alone had any power, Mel would be a pillar of salt about now.

"No, I had two children. I should know that, you insolent child. Matthew was born right after Phillip and I were mated. He was a lovely boy, but not a daughter, so we had your mother. This was before the High Council decided that we should only have daughters and, as we lived forever, that only having one child would not over-populate the kingdom. I didn't think about the consequences at the time or how it would affect future generations, so I agreed. I'm so sorry every day that I agreed to such a cruel law. Had I known what it would do to my family, I would never have done it."

"But that doesn't explain why you were at the shelter. How did you know I was there?" Sara asked.

"Dawn, your mother, had told Matt that she needed money. He was to meet her somewhere with it, and she would give him something to hold in trust for it. He didn't know about you… none of us did, actually. He came to me right before he was to leave to say he was very ill. Something in the human world had made him sick. You see, because he wasn't female, he could be hurt and killed like all other mortals. He didn't get better. A week after he came to me, he was dead. He told me all about the meeting and the arrangement that he was to bring her money for something she had for him. I went to look for her to tell her what had happened. I couldn't leave him…not then. I had her money but was hoping I could bring her to the castle to live out her days. Matt had loved her so much, you see. I couldn't find her, but there was a trail, a signature that led me to the shelter. Now, I can only assume it was you."

"Do you have a tattoo, darling? Not the one Melody gave you, but another?" James asked her.

"Why do you want to know?" Sara asked suspiciously.

"Where is it? I'd like to see it if you don't mind." He didn't answer her question, but these people had saved her life, so Sara pulled up the sleeve of her t-shirt.

With her shields down, the tattoo was visible for anyone to see. It was the same as Melody's but with a set of crossed swords across the base of the tree. It, too, was in full color. James looked at the mark for a long time and then threw back his head and laughed. He had tears streaming down his cheeks; his happiness was so great. It was a good long time before he could talk.

"Mine is different from Mel's. I have the swords. I never

thought about it when Mel touched me to mark me. I'd hidden it for so long...I guess I never thought about it anymore," she explained.

"Yes," Phillip said, "you would. The swords belong to me. I was a member of the Royal Guard when I met Elizabeth. The crest for a member of the Royal Guard back then was a pair of crossed claymores, and nothing else. It looks to me like the combination of the two Royal Crests is what you carry. That would explain your power and your ability to fight. You are my blood, Sara Temple. You are a true immortal. Welcome to the family."

Then Phillip stood before the large vampire and demanded, "Now there is the matter of you, my fine sir. What are your intentions for my granddaughter?"

CHAPTER TWENTY-FOUR

"I want you, Sara. I want to be buried deep inside of you soon," Aaron whispered to her.

"Yes, please. But I need a bath. Will you bathe with me, Aaron? Wash me clean for you, get me all wet? Wet for you?" She purred at him.

Aaron growled at her from deep in his throat. He could already smell that she was wet for him, and it had nothing to do with the bathtub. He carried her to his lair, down under the deepest part of the house. When they entered his bedroom, he turned the taps on to the tub, never taking his hands away from the delectable woman in his arms.

"Sara, I want to feel you against me, against my skin. How fast can you get out of these clothes, love?" Suddenly, they were both naked. She had removed both their clothes with a thought. Oh, he could get used to this.

"Me too. I want to taste you, Aaron. I want to bite you, please? I want to taste your blood in my mouth, on my tongue. I want to give you the same pleasure you give me when you drink from me. Tell me how."

He looked down at her. Was she asking to bond with him? Did she know what her bite would do to them as a couple?

"Sara, do you know what you are asking me?"

"Yes, I want to be yours for eternity. Please, tell me what to do." His cock hardened against her belly. He knew he wouldn't last long.

"Sara, God, I can't wait on a bath. It has to be now."

Aaron sat on the edge of the bed and pulled her to his lap, her legs wrapped around him, and so that her chest met his. He needed to be inside of her when she bit him, and this was the perfect position for her to reach his vein, and he, her pussy. He was throbbing with his need for her. He reached between her legs to see if she was wet enough to take him quickly, and she soaked his fingers, drew them into her with the slightest movement. He could feel his release gathering up, ready to explode forth. Before he got any more desperate, he lifted her up and lowered her slowly onto his cock.

Inch by inch, she took him in, her heat and cream bathing him. He looked down at them, watched as she took him in, as he entered her. Her pussy widening for him, the tightness and heat overwhelming; nothing had ever felt this good. When he was finally seated inside, he moved up into her deeper.

"God, Aaron, don't move, or I'll come now. Show me. Show me what to do so we can make love. Fast."

"Lick...lick my pulse, feel where it is." When her tongue began its journey down his neck, he thought he'd pass out from the sensations. She was making him wild with his need to take her. "Oh, God, Sara, that's it. Bathe it with your tongue. I'm going to...oh, baby, please. I'm going to open my vein for you. When I do, I want you to take as much of me as you can. When you put your mouth over me and suck, I'm going to bite you. There will... we need to exchange our blood at the same time we climax for us to be truly bonded. Hurry, baby, or I won't last."

Sara laved her tongue over the fast-beating pulse once more and bit sharply into him. He moved her aside gently as he extended a sharp claw at the end of his index finger. With a quick slice, his blood poured forth. This time, when she laid her mouth over the pulse, his blood filled her mouth. When she suckled at the opening, pulling more of him into her, he screamed her name out with his release. He rolled them over, turning them around, and slammed her down on the bed onto her back, pumping into her pussy deeper and harder. He bit her then, rolling her into her own release like a tornado touching down. Every part of his body felt it. When she started to come again, he began pumping his seed into her, harder and harder with every stroke, until he emptied himself deep inside her.

Aaron rolled over onto his back, pulling her with him. He was spent and had used the last of his reserves just doing that simple task. He held her close to his body by the weight of his arm and nothing more. Soon they both were asleep.

~~~

After a short three-hour nap, they refilled the tub and cuddled in the warm water. "You know, now that we've mated, you're a true immortal as well," Sara said. Aaron watched as she lifted her leg high out of the water and ran the sponge down the length. Staring at her, he nearly missed what she was saying. "Will I change into a vampire now?"

"Honestly, I don't know. It's hard to say what your body will do if anything at all. However, I have to tell you, the thought of you having fangs is really sexy."

As she was sitting between his legs, it didn't take much to show how sexy he thought it was. He was hard every time he was near her and now wasn't any exception.

"Is all you can think about sex?" she groused at him.

Aaron thought about it and grinned, but didn't put forth too much effort and answered her. "Yes. Of course, but only when you're around." His smile was pure sin.

"Good save and good answer." She turned around to his body and straddled his lap. She began to move up and down, back and forth across his erection, riding him. He reached out to lift her breast, pulling her nipple into his mouth, sucking hard.

"Sara, I want to bite you. I want to bite your nipple and nurse from you." She moaned hard and deep at his need.

Sara didn't answer him with words but lifted herself up and

over him. She reached down and pulled him up, stroking his cock once, and fit him into her. She slid herself down onto him, seating herself fully before she began rocking against him again. Leaning forward, she lifted and gave him her breast, moaning loudly when he again pulled her nipple into his warmth. He looked into her eyes, seeing her trust, and bit. She began bucking hard down on him, nearly throwing herself off until he grabbed her hips, grinding her down harder, helping her reach her climax. He drew her essences into him, suckling at her nipple like a babe at the breast. He came with a groan, spewing into her again and again.

CHAPTER TWENTY-FIVE

"Duncan, do you think you and I can manage a few people over tonight? I think maybe ten at the most. I don't know how to go about it, but Aaron said you could handle anything," Sara asked Duncan the next morning.

Aaron had said no such thing, but she wanted Duncan to like her, and it was just a little fib. They were to go to the castle for a ceremony, then back here for drinks and whatever Duncan could dream up.

"Why, of course, My Lady. Anything you'd like. I understand you have found your family."

"Yes, it seems as though I'm the queen's cousin." Sara grinned at him. "She wants me to work with her in the Royal Court, as her advisor. She's thousands of years older than me, and she wants my advice. What on earth do I tell her, I ask you? Oh well, but the first thing I did tell her was to abolish that stupid rule about only having one child. Maybe she'll find a mate again and have hundreds of rug rats for me to play with. I can be the wonderful aunt, don't you think, Duncan?"

"Yes, My Lady. You would be wonderful at anything you set your head to," he said in all seriousness.

She grinned. She so loved the way he butchered the sayings. She seldom corrected him. She wasn't sure how he would take it yet.

~~~

Sara had taken time to dress and arm herself. She was dressed in her full armor, chain maille and all, as she'd been asked to by Phillip...err, Granddad to do. He said that he'd like to honor her as his granddaughter and as a Royal Guard. He was so excited about it that she couldn't refuse him.

When she'd fled the castle four years ago, she had hidden this dress uniform away, thinking never to wear it again. Now here she was, not only dressed again in her first uniform but waiting to perform a ceremony of sorts.

Sara's armory was a chain maille sleeveless vest called a cuirass that fit her like a glove, molding over her back and breasts, ending at her small waist. Her greaves were made of a superior metal that was made especially for her, protecting her lower legs from vicious kicks and blows aimed to take her feet from under her. Her shoes, the softest material produced in the castle, gripped any surface she stood on. Whether it was wet, dry or icy slick, they held her fast. Her gauntlets were just fingerless gloves, made of leatherlike material that was by far more superior to that of its counterpart, which ended a few inches above her wrist, protecting her hands from any nicks. She carried a flail around her waist, the spiked ball strapped to her leg with a quick release belt to hold it safely against her leg. At her back, she wore a war mallet, its head blunt, and its nail sharp. In her hand was her favored weapon, a sword that looked a great deal like a highlander claymore, but a much smaller version to fit her hand and stature.

All her armament had been charmed with magic. Mel had it fashioned for her, and she was the one who had given it the extra bit of magic to keep her friend safe. The other blades on her person were hidden from view but easily accessible to her. She was exactly what she looked like, a beautiful, trained killer.

When Sara walked into the throne room later that night, she found Sherman standing on the seat of her throne, prying jewels out of the headboard. Mel was nowhere to be found. He'd even put on one of her crowns. It was actually too feminine to be worn by a man. Somehow, though, it suited him perfectly. She hated the man, all that he stood for, and what he had done to her and to those she loved.

"What the hell do you think you're doing?" Sara asked, startling him to have him nearly fall. "You are by far the stupidest man I've ever met, do you know that? I've always wondered if you need to carry around a timer. I wondered if you needed something to remind you to inhale and exhale, so you don't pass out. Where's Mel?"

"My mate? How the hell should I know?" he snarled back. "And you know what? I could care less. I'm taking what is owed me. I was so hoping that bitch would come in, but this is so much the better. I can ruin that fucking vampire and Melody at the same time by your death."

With a small nod of his head, someone came at Sara from behind. She knew he had been there, awaiting Sherman's signal. She turned and sliced the man in two, her blade catching him off guard. She was sure he'd not known she was aware of him. Before the man fell to the floor, four more came at her.

Sara was incredibly strong and fast, her speed no match for the men, mere children in their stance and ability to fight, especially someone as talented as she. She worked her way through them in three minutes. When she turned back to the man on the throne, she smirked at him until she noticed that he'd taken Aaron as a captive. He must have entered when she was fighting. Damn it, where was Mel?

"Sara, dear, I have something of yours," Sherman said in a sing-song voice. "And I plan to kill him slowly. Maybe I'll stake him in the sun to die. I believe I would enjoy that to the very end."

"You'll die. I will relish killing you very slowly, you filthy bastard." Her voice was calm while inside, she was seething with barely suppressed rage.

Sara had been distracted, or Sherman would never have

gotten as close to Aaron as he had. In those few precious seconds, she was defending herself, he'd attacked.

Sherman worked his way to the door to the main hall. He was completely hidden by Aaron, who hung limp in his arm. He had a blade at his throat and his arm about his waist. Sara, a blade in each hand, stood before them, blocking his exit.

"You'll not get away from here with him. You have to know that. Even if you were to get out of this room alive, I would hunt you down for the coward you are. And mark my word, you will not go so easily. Let him go now. Or are you so afraid of me, Shermie, that you need to hide behind someone?" She had not one nick on her flawless skin. "So afraid of me that you send others to do what you know you cannot? Like, defeat me?"

Sara looked at the man she loved, and her heart swelled at the look he gave her. He was smiling. He trusted her.

"I don't want to hurt you. I don't know what to do," she whispered to his mind.

"Of course you do, love. You need to kill him. And the sooner, the better. I want nothing more than to peel each piece of the sexy armaments from that delicious body of yours, kissing each exposed succulent inch of you as I do." She suddenly realized what he was doing. She felt more relaxed, less terrified.

"I love you, Aaron. So very much."

"I know that. And why wouldn't you? I'm awesome." She heard his laughter as it raced along her spine.

Maybe if she pissed Shermie off enough, she thought, he'd make a mistake, and she could overpower him. But her prime objective was to get him away from Aaron.

Sara felt Mel seconds before she came into the room, and when the door crashed with a resounding boom against the tapestry on the wall behind it, she made her move. She lunged at Sherman and took his blade away from him, freeing Aaron in the process.

With a quick flick of her power, she threw Sherman to the

floor and bound him to it. As she walked toward him, pulling her claymore from its sheath, she stripped him of Mel's crown and jewels with a bit more magic.

"Oh, Shermie boy, now what do you think?" Sara asked as she stood over the man. "What did you say about staking my mate to the ground? Oh yeah, I can see by the look on your face that you'd have no idea about that. Maybe I should let him drain you...no, I'm thinking that might leave a bad taste in his mouth." She put the point of the claymore at his throat and held it there. She didn't apply enough pressure to draw blood, but she wanted to.

"Sara, honey, I have something I'd like to say to my mate if you don't mind? I believe it will make it easier for you to finish what you so desperately need to do," Mel said just behind her. In a voice clear and distinct, she heard Mel say, "Sherman, I denounce you before all that are assembled before us."

The second the words left Mel's mouth, not even echoing throughout the cavernous room, Sara rammed the blade home. The force of it nearly severed his head from his body a mere second after Mel stripped him of his immortality through their bond. Before her blade could touch the floor through his neck, blood splattered everywhere, and Sherman disappeared.

CHAPTER TWENTY-SIX

"So, is he dead?" Sara looked at Aaron and sighed at his question.

Was he? She didn't know. He'd been such a huge part of her life until now she wasn't sure what to believe about him. She knew that her sword should have severed his head, but he'd disappeared.

Sara and Aaron had gone back to his bedroom in the house's sublevels, where they had slept for most of the day. Her armaments lay scattered all over the room, as were his clothes, or at least what was left of them. She and Aaron were now lying on his big bed.

"I really don't know. Shermie has a great deal of magical resources to fall back on. I can't feel him, but that could only mean that he's hiding behind his magic. Black magic is so different than mine."

Sara wanted to believe him dead but knew that he'd show up again. He hadn't finished with them yet, especially Mel. When Mel had taken away his immortality, she'd literally taken away his livelihood.

Sherman was without money, without a home, and injured, so where would he go? Mel had been his mate, and his means to money or whatever else he desired, as well as things he just wanted because he could. She could only imagine what he'd do now.

"I think he's alive," Sara reasoned. "I'm not sure why, but I do. He would have had a backup plan. He was a lot of things, but he wasn't stupid. I'm sure that he had monies enough to keep him comfortable for a while, but it won't last. He probably had homes throughout this world and maybe a few on the other side, though I don't see him showing up there too soon. He'd need to gather his strength, to maybe lay low for a time until he was fit, stronger." She looked over at the man she loved with all her being. "I'll protect you, no matter what. I'll keep you safe in my life and in my heart. This household, these people...I don't know what I'd do without them, without you."

Aaron rolled over to blanket himself across her body; she could feel him hard across her. "I love you, Sara. I never thought to love or be loved in my life. When you stepped up to me that long ago summer evening, I thought I was looking at a beautiful woman. Now I realize how wrong I was. I was looking into the eyes of my life, my future, and my mate. I was looking at the only woman I'd ever love, ever want to love. Sara, will you become my mate in the tradition of my kind?"

Tears streamed down her face as she looked up at him. Her throat closed up around the lump that had settled there. Sara nodded to him.

He reached beyond the bed to the side table and pulled open the drawer to it. Inside there was a bejeweled dagger and a box. Aaron pulled out the dagger and slipped it under the pillow. The box he laid beside her.

"For many centuries, our kind had chosen a mate based on their ability to feed from them. There was never a time when we thought to mate with another simply to have the pleasure of being with that one person for all of eternity. Love was never a part of it. I've known many men who would shun the idea of taking a mate, especially a human mate." She watched as he opened the box as he spoke. "But none of them had the love or the power of that love to show them what they were missing. I love you, Sara Temple MacManus. I'll love you until the end of all time and beyond."

Aaron kissed her then, deep and strong. His tongue stroked hers with possessiveness and heat. Sara moaned long and felt his responding groan rumble through his skin.

"Aaron, please. I need you inside of me now." Shifting slightly, he surged his cock deep inside of her hard and fast, her wetness making the slide easy. Lifting her legs up, she encircled them tightly around his slim hips and, using his ass as leverage, lifted herself up to meet his downward thrust.

"Baby, we have...Christ, but you're hot. Baby, please, we need to complete this." He rocked, again and again, sweat beading on his forehead. He finally pushed his weight onto hers, stopping any movement.

"Aaron, no!" Try as she might, she couldn't make him move again. Aaron nuzzled hard against her throat, and she gave it to him. Anything to get him to finish her.

"We have to...Sara, will you drink from me? I'll...I want to fuck you. Stop moving, damn it." Laughter laced his voice. She smiled and squeezed her thighs tighter around him. His groan of approval made her laugh out loud. "I'll cut my vein, and when you come, I want you to drink from the wound. I'll bite you at the same time. We have to come at the same time," he admonished her.

"If you're as close as I am, then it won't be a problem. Hurry, please hurry." To prove her point, she tightened her muscles around his cock again.

He cut into his throat and surged into her hard and fast. His body pumped hard into hers, and she welcomed each thrust.

"Now, baby, now!" With a final push, he took her over the edge, and she screamed as the most powerful orgasm ripped through her. As she felt him lick her pulse, she fitted her mouth over his wound and sucked. Stars burst behind her lids at the sensations rioting through her. When he sank his teeth deep into her, she came again, convulsing and tightening around his cock as she came over and over.

~~~

When it was possible for him to move again, Aaron shifted to his side, pulling her with him. His body had never felt so relaxed and sated before. Breathing deeply, he pulled her scent into his lungs, tasting her on his tongue, feeling her throughout his body.

"Sara? Are you all right?" He smiled as she moaned instead of answering. He kissed the top of her head and reached for the small box he'd put on her pillow earlier. "I have a gift for you. Do you want it?"

"Does it involve sex? If it does, you'll need to give me a few more...I don't know, years to recuperate." Stretching, she looked up at him. "I love you."

"And I, you. Marry me, Sara. Be my wife as well as my mate." He slipped the diamond ring on the ring finger of her left hand and kissed it. He hoped she'd say yes, but with Sara, one just never knew.

"Oh, Aaron, oh my...I love you." Each word was punctuated with a kiss to his face, his chest, his neck. When she got to his mouth, he stopped her progress with a hand to the back of her head and deepened the kiss.

"Sara, love, you didn't answer me," he whispered against her mouth. Spending an eternity exploring this woman might not be enough, he decided. Then again, it might just kill him.

"Oh, yes, yes, yes, yes, yes, I'll marry you."

Before You Go…

HELP AN AUTHOR

write a review

THANK YOU!

Share your voice and help guide other readers to these wonderful books. Even if it's only a line or two, your reviews help readers discover the author's books so they can continue creating stories that you'll love. Log in to your favorite retailer and leave a review. Thank you.

AWARD WINNING, BESTSELLING AUTHOR

Kathi Barton, a winner of the Pinnacle Book Achievement Award and a best-selling author on Amazon and All Romance books, lives in Nashport, Ohio, with her husband, Paul. When not creating new worlds and romance, Kathi and her husband enjoy camping and going to auctions. She can also be seen at county fairs with her husband, who is an artist and potter.

Her muse, a cross between Jimmy Stewart and Hugh Jackman, brings her stories to life for her readers in a way that has them coming back time and again for more. Her favorite genre is paranormal romance, with a great deal of spice. You can visit Kathi on line and drop her an email if you'd like. She loves hearing from her fans. aaronskiss@gmail.com.

Follow Kathi on her blog: http://kathisbartonauthor.blogspot.com/

Made in the USA
Middletown, DE
07 September 2021

47047489R00132